You are the sole survivor of a devastating attack on the monastery where you were learning the skills of the Kai Lords. You swear vengeance on the Darklords for the massacre of the Kai warriors, and with a sudden flash of insight you know what you must do. You must set off on a perilous journey to the capital city to warn the King of the terrible threat that faces his people. For you are now the last of the Kai—you are now LONE WOLF.

JOE DEVER is a contributing editor to *White Dwarf*, Britain's leading fantasy games magazine. The Lone Wolf series is the culmination of seven years of research and involvement with the unique world of fantasy. He is currently at work on a huge compendium based on the world of Magnamund.

GARY CHALK was working as a children's book illustrator when he became involved in adventure gaming, an interest which eventually led to the creation of several successful games. He is the inventor/illustrator of some of Britain's biggest-selling fantasy games.

Book 1

Flight from the Dark

Joe Dever and Gary Chalk

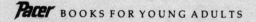

Pacer BOOKS FOR YOUNG ADULTS

a member of the Putnam Publishing Group

NEW YORK

FLIGHT FROM THE DARK

Pacer Books are published by
The Putnam Young Readers Group
51 Madison Avenue
New York, New York 10010

Distributed by The Berkley Publishing Group

ISBN: 0-425-08436-1
RL: 7.7

Pacer is a trademark belonging to The Putnam Publishing Group

The name "BERKLEY" and the stylized "B" with design are
trademarks belonging to Berkley Publishing Corporation.
Reprinted by arrangement with Sparrow Books, an
imprint of the Hutchinson Publishing Group.
PRINTED IN THE UNITED STATES OF AMERICA
First Pacer Printing January 1985
Second Pacer Printing April 1985

To Mel and Yin

ACTION CHART

KAI DISCIPLINES

NOTES

1	
2	
3	
4	
5	
6	

You can have 6th Discipline if you have completed Book 1 successfull•

WEAPONS (maximum 2 Weapons)

1	
2	

If combat entered holding Weapon and appropriate Weaponskill + 2CS
If combat entered carrying no Weapon —4CS.

BACKPACK (maximum 8 articles)

ITEMS	MEALS
	—3 EP if no Meal available when instructed to eat.
Can be discarded or changed when not in combat.	

SPECIAL ITEMS	BELT POUCH Containing Gold Crowns (maximum 50)

CS = COMBAT SKILL   EP = ENDURANCE POINTS

COMBAT SKILL	ENDURANCE POINTS
	Can never go above initial score. 0 = dead

COMBAT RECORD

ENDURANCE POINTS		ENDURANCE POINTS
LONE WOLF	COMBAT RATIO	ENEMY
LONE WOLF	COMBAT RATIO	ENEMY
LONE WOLF	COMBAT RATIO	ENEMY
LONE WOLF	COMBAT RATIO	ENEMY
LONE WOLF	COMBAT RATIO	ENEMY
LONE WOLF		

ACTION CHART

KAI DISCIPLINES   NOTES

1	
2	
3	
4	
5	
6	

You can have 6th Discipline if you have completed Book 1 successfu

WEAPONS (maximum 2 Weapons)

1	
2	

If combat entered holding Weapon and appropriate Weaponskill + 2C
If combat entered carrying no Weapon —4CS.

BACKPACK (maximum 8 articles)

ITEMS	MEALS
Can be discarded or changed when not in combat.	—3 EP if no Meal available when instructed to eat.

SPECIAL ITEMS	BELT POUCH Containing Gold Crowns (maximum 50)

CS = COMBAT SKILL   EP = ENDURANCE POINTS

COMBAT SKILL		ENDURANCE POINTS
		Can never go above initial score. 0 = dead

COMBAT RECORD

ENDURANCE POINTS		ENDURANCE POINTS
LONE WOLF	COMBAT RATIO	ENEMY
LONE WOLF	COMBAT RATIO	ENEMY
LONE WOLF	COMBAT RATIO	ENEMY
LONE WOLF	COMBAT RATIO	ENEMY
LONE WOLF	COMBAT RATIO	ENEMY
LONE WOLF	CO	

(Spare copy of *Action Chart*)

THE STORY SO FAR . . .

In the northern land of Sommerlund, it has been the custom for many centuries to send the children of the Warrior Lords to the monastery of Kai. There they are taught the skills and disciplines of their noble fathers.

The Kai monks are masters of their art, and the children in their charge love and respect them in spite of the hardships of their training. For one day when they have finally learnt the secret skills of the Kai, they will return to their homes equipped in mind and body to defend themselves against the constant threat of war from the Darklords of the west.

In olden times, during the Age of the Black Moon, the Darklords waged war on Sommerlund. The conflict was a long and bitter trial of strength that ended in victory for the Sommlending at the great battle of Maakengorge. King Ulnar and the allies of Durenor broke the Darklord armies at the pass of Moytura and forced them back into the bottomless abyss of Maakengorge. Vashna, mightiest of the Darklords, was slain upon the sword of King Ulnar, called 'Sommerswerd', the sword of the sun. Since that age, the Darklords have vowed vengeance upon Sommerlund and the House of Ulnar.

Now it is in the morning of the feast of Fehmarn, when all of the Kai Lords are present at the monastery for the celebrations. Suddenly a great black cloud comes from out of the western skies. So many are the numbers of the black-winged beasts that fill the sky, that the sun is completely hidden. The Darklords, ancient enemy of the Sommlending, are attacking. War has begun.

On this fateful morning, you, Silent Wolf (the name given to you by the Kai) have been sent to collect firewood in the forest as a punishment for your inattention in class. As you are preparing to return, you see to your horror a vast cloud of black leathery creatures swoop down and engulf the monastery.

Dropping the wood, you race to the battle that has already begun. But in the unnatural dark, you stumble and strike your head on a low tree branch. As you lose consciousness, the last thing that you see in the poor light are the walls of the monastery crashing to the ground.

Many hours pass before you awake. With tears in your eyes you now survey the scene of destruction. Raising your face to the clear sky, you swear vengeance on the Darklords for the massacre of the Kai warriors, and with a sudden flash of realization you know what you must do. You must set off on a perilous journey to the capital city to warn the King of the terrible threat that now faces his people. For you are now the last of the Kai – you are now the *Lone Wolf*.

THE GAME RULES

You keep a record of your adventure on the *Action Chart* that you will find in the front of this book. For further adventuring you can copy out the chart yourself or get it photocopied.

During your training as a Kai Lord you have developed fighting prowess – COMBAT SKILL and physical stamina – ENDURANCE. Before you set off on your adventure you need to measure how effective your training has been. To do this take a pencil and, with your eyes closed, point with the blunt end of it on to the *Random Number Table* on the last page of this book. If you pick *0* it counts as zero.

The first number that you pick from the *Random Number Table* in this way represents your COMBAT SKILL. Add 10 to the number you picked and write the total in the COMBAT SKILL section of your *Action Chart*. (ie, if your pencil fell on *4* in the *Random Number Table* you would write in a COMBAT SKILL of 14.) When you fight, your COMBAT SKILL will be pitted against that of your enemy. A high score in this section is therefore very desirable.

The second number that you pick from the *Random Number Table* represents your powers of ENDURANCE. Add 20 to this number and write the total in the ENDURANCE section of your *Action Chart*. (ie, if your pencil fell on the number 6 on the *Random Number Table* you would have 26 ENDURANCE points.)

If you are wounded in combat you will lose ENDURANCE points. If at any time your ENDURANCE points fall to zero, you are dead and the adventure is over. Lost ENDURANCE points can be regained during the course of the adventure, but your number of ENDURANCE points can never go above the number with which you start your adventure.

KAI DISCIPLINES

Over the centuries, the Kai monks have mastered the skills of the warrior. These skills are known as the Kai Disciplines, and they are taught to all Kai Lords. You have learnt only *five* of the skills listed below. The choice of which five skills these are, is for you to make. As all of the disciplines will be of use to you at some point on your perilous quest, pick your five with care. The correct use of a discipline at the right time can save your life.

When you have chosen your five disciplines, enter them in the Kai Discipline section of your *Action Chart*.

Camouflage

This discipline enables a Kai Lord to blend in with his surroundings. In the countryside, he can hide undetected among trees and rocks and pass close to an enemy without being seen. In a town or city, it enables him to look and sound like a native of that area, and can help him to find shelter or a safe hiding place.

If you choose this skill, write 'Camouflage' on your *Action Chart*.

Hunting

This skill ensures that a Kai Lord will never starve in the wild. He will always be able to hunt for food for himself except in areas of wasteland and desert. The skill also enables a Kai Lord to be able to move stealthily when stalking his prey.

If you choose this skill, write 'Hunting: no need for a Meal when instructed to eat' on your *Action Chart*.

Sixth Sense

This skill may warn a Kai Lord of imminent danger. It may also reveal the true purpose of a stranger or strange object encountered in your adventure.

If you choose this skill, write 'Sixth Sense' on your *Action Chart*.

Tracking

This skill enables a Kai Lord to make the correct choice of a path in the wild, to discover the location of a person or object in a town or city and to read the secrets of footprints or tracks.

If you choose this skill, write 'Tracking' on your *Action Chart*.

Healing

This discipline can be used to restore ENDURANCE points lost in combat. If you possess this skill you may restore 1 ENDURANCE point to your total for every numbered section of the book you pass through in which you are not involved in combat. (This is only to be used after your ENDURANCE has fallen below its original level.) Remember that your ENDURANCE cannot rise above its original level.

If you choose this skill, write 'Healing: + 1 ENDURANCE point for each section without combat' on your *Action Chart*.

Weaponskill

Upon entering the Kai monastery, each initiate is taught to master one type of weapon. If Weaponskill is to be one of your Kai Disciplines, pick a number in the usual way from the *Random Number Table* on the last page of the book, and then find the corresponding weapon from the list below. This is the weapon in which you have skill. When you enter combat carrying this weapon, you add 2 points to your COMBAT SKILL.

0 = DAGGER

1 = SPEAR

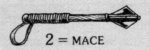

2 = MACE

16

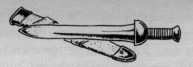

3 = SHORT SWORD

4 = WARHAMMER

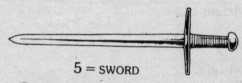

5 = SWORD

6 = AXE

7 = SWORD

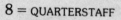

8 = QUARTERSTAFF

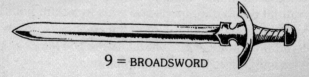

9 = BROADSWORD

The fact that you are skilled with a weapon does not mean you set out on the adventure carrying that particular weapon. However, you will have opportunities to acquire weapons in the course of your adventures. If you pick the axe, you are lucky enough to be skilled in the one weapon Lone Wolf is carrying from the start of the adventure. (Explained fully in Equipment section.)

You cannot carry more than 2 weapons. If you choose this skill, write 'Weaponskill in —————: + 2 COMBAT SKILL points if this weapon carried' on your Action Chart.

Mindshield

The Darklords and many of the evil creatures in their command have the ability to attack you using their Mindforce. The Kai Discipline of Mindshield prevents you from losing any ENDURANCE points when subjected to this form of attack.

If you choose this skill, write 'Mindshield: no points lost when attacked by Mindblast' on your Action Chart.

Mindblast

This enables a Kai Lord to attack an enemy using the force of his mind. It can be used at the same time as normal combat weapons and adds two extra points to your COMBAT SKILL. Not all the creatures encountered on this adventure will be harmed by Mindblast. You will be told if a creature is immune.

f you choose this skill, write 'Mindblast: + 2 COMBAT SKILL points' on your *Action Chart*.

Animal Kinship

This skill enables a Kai Lord to communicate with some animals and to be able to guess the intentions of others.

If you choose this skill, write 'Animal Kinship' on your *Action Chart*.

Mind Over Matter

Mastery of this discipline enables a Kai Lord to move small objects with his powers of concentration.

If you choose this skill, write 'Mind Over Matter' on your *Action Chart*.

If you successfully complete the mission as set in Book 1 of Lone Wolf, you may add a further Kai Discipline of your choice to your *Action Chart* in Book 2. This additional skill, together with your five other skills and any Special Items that you have picked up in Book 1, may then be used in the next adventure of the Lone Wolf series which is called *Fire on the Water*.

EQUIPMENT

You are dressed in the green tunic and cloak of a Kai initiate. You have little with you to arm yourself for survival.

All you possess is an Axe (note under Weapons on your *Action Chart*) and a Backpack containing 1 Meal (note under Meals on your *Action Chart*). Hanging from your waist is a leather pouch containing Gold Crowns. To find out how many, pick a number from the *Random Number Table*. This number equals the number of Gold Crowns you possess at the start of the adventure. (Note the number in the Belt Pouch section of the *Action Chart*.)

You discover amongst the smoking ruins of the monastery, a Map of Sommerlund (note under Special Items on the *Action Chart*) showing the capital city of Holmgard and the land of Durenor, far to the east. You place the Map inside your tunic for safety.

You also find one of the following:

1 = SWORD (Weapons)
2 = HELMET (Special Items). This adds 2 ENDURANCE
   points to your total

3 = TWO MEALS (Meals)

4 = CHAINMAIL WAISTCOAT (Special Items). This adds
   4 ENDURANCE points to your total

5 = MACE (Weapons)

6 = HEALING POTION (Backpack Item). This can restore 4 ENDURANCE points to your total, when swallowed after combat. You only have enough for one dose.

7 = QUARTERSTAFF (Weapons)

8 = SPEAR (Weapons)

9 = 12 GOLD CROWNS (Belt Pouch)

0 = BROADSWORD (Weapons)

To discover which of the above you find, you must pick a number from the *Random Number Table* and find the corresponding article on the list. Note this on your *Action Chart*, under the heading given in brackets, and make a note of any effect it may have on your ENDURANCE points.

How to carry equipment

Now that you have your equipment, the following list shows you how it is carried. You don't need to make notes but you can refer back to this list in the course of your adventure.

1 = SWORD – carried in the hand.

2 = HELMET – worn on the head.

3 = FOOD – placed in the Backpack.

4 = CHAINMAIL WAISTCOAT – worn on the body.
5 = MACE – carried in the hand.
6 = HEALING POTION – carried in the Backpack.
7 = QUARTERSTAFF – carried in the hand.
8 = SPEAR – carried in the hand.
9 = GOLD CROWNS – carried in the Belt Pouch.
0 = BROADSWORD – carried in the hand.

How much can you carry?

Weapons
The maximum number of weapons that you may carry is *two*.

Backpack Items
These must be stored in your Backpack. Because space is limited, you may only keep a maximum of eight articles, including Meals, in your Backpack at any one time.

Special Items
Special Items are not carried in the Backpack. When you discover a Special Item, you will be told how to carry it.

Gold Crowns
These are always carried in the Belt Pouch. It will hold a maximum of fifty crowns.

Food
Food is carried in your Backpack. Each Meal counts as one item.

Any item that may be of use and can be picked up on your adventure and entered on your *Action Chart* is given capital letters in the text. Unless you are told it is a Special Item, carry it in your Backpack.

How to use your equipment

Weapons

Weapons aid you in combat. If you have the Kai Discipline of Weaponskill and the correct weapon, it adds 2 points to your COMBAT SKILL. If you enter a combat with no weapons, deduct 4 points from your COMBAT SKILL and fight with your bare hands. If you find a weapon during the adventure, you may pick it up and use it (Remember you can only carry two weapons at once.)

Backpack Items

During your travels you will discover various useful items which you may wish to keep. (Remember you can only carry eight items in your Backpack at once.) You may exchange or discard them at any point when you are not involved in combat.

Special Items

Each Special Item has a particular purpose or effect. You may be told this when the item is discovered, or it may be revealed to you as the adventure progresses.

Gold Crowns

The local currency is the Crown, which is a small gold coin. Gold Crowns can be used on your adventure to pay for transport, food or even as a bribe! Many of the creatures that you will encounter possess Gold Crowns, or have them hidden in their lairs. Whenever you kill a creature, you may take any Gold Crowns that it has and put them in your Belt Pouch.

23

Food

You will need to eat regularly during your adventure. If you do not have any food when you are instructed to eat a Meal, you will lose 3 ENDURANCE points. If you have chosen the Kai Discipline of Hunting as one of your five skills, you will not need to tick off a Meal when instructed to eat.

Healing Potion

This can restore 4 ENDURANCE points to your total when swallowed after combat. There is only enough for one dose. If you discover any other potions during the adventure, you will be told then of their effect. All Healing Potions are Backpack Items.

RULES FOR COMBAT

There will be occasions on your adventure when you have to fight an enemy. The enemy's COMBAT SKILL and ENDURANCE points are given in the text. Lone Wolf's aim in the combat is to kill the enemy by reducing his ENDURANCE points to zero while losing as few ENDURANCE points as possible himself.

At the start of a combat, enter Lone Wolf's and the enemy's ENDURANCE points in the appropriate boxes on the Combat Record section of your *Action Chart*.

The sequence for combat is as follows.

1. Add any extra points gained through your Kai Disciplines to your current COMBAT SKILL total.

2. Subtract the COMBAT SKILL of your enemy from this total. The result is your *Combat Ratio*. Enter it on the *Action Chart*.

24

Example

Lone Wolf (COMBAT SKILL 15) is ambushed by a Winged Devil (COMBAT SKILL 20). He is not given the opportunity to evade combat, but must stand and fight as the creature swoops down on him. Lone Wolf has the Kai Discipline of Mindblast, so he adds 2 points to his COMBAT SKILL giving a total COMBAT SKILL of 17.

He subtracts the Winged Devil's COMBAT SKILL from his own, giving a *Combat Ratio* of -3. $(17 - 20 = -3)$. -3 is noted on the *Action Chart* as the *Combat Ratio*.

3. When you have your *Combat Ratio*, pick a number from the *Random Number Table*.

4. Turn to the *Combat Results Table* on the inside back cover of the book. Along the top of the chart are shown the *Combat Ratio* numbers. Find the number that is the same as your *Combat Ratio* and cross-reference it with the random number that you have picked (the random numbers appear on the side of the chart). You now have the number of ENDURANCE points lost by both Lone Wolf and his enemy in this round of combat. (*E* represents points lost by the enemy; *LW* represents points lost by Lone Wolf.)

Example

The *Combat Ratio* between Lone Wolf and Winged Devil has been established as -3. If the number taken from the *Random Number Table* is a 6, then the result of the first round of combat is:

Lone Wolf loses 3 ENDURANCE points
Winged Devil loses 6 ENDURANCE points

5. On the *Action Chart*, mark the changes in ENDURANCE points to the participants in the combat.

6. Unless otherwise instructed, or unless you have an option to evade, the next round of combat now starts.

7. Repeat the sequence from Stage 3.

This process of combat continues until the ENDURANCE points of either the enemy or Lone Wolf are reduced to zero, at which point the one with the zero score is declared dead. If Lone Wolf is dead, the adventure is over. If the enemy is dead, Lone Wolf proceeds but with his ENDURANCE points reduced .

A summary of Combat Rules appears on the page after the *Random Number Table*.

Evasion of combat

During your adventure you may be given the chance to evade combat. If you have already engaged in a round of combat and decide to evade, calculate the combat for that round in the usual manner. All points lost by the enemy as a result of that round are ignored, and you make your escape. Only Lone Wolf may lose ENDURANCE points during that round, but then that is the risk of running away! You may only evade if the text of the particular section allows you to do so.

KAI WISDOM

Your mission will be one of great danger, for the Darklords and their servants are a cruel and fierce enemy who give and expect no mercy. Use the map on the back cover of the book to help you steer a correct course for the capital. Make notes as you progress through the story, for they will be of great help in future adventures.

Many things that you find will aid you during the adventure. Some Special Items will be of use in future LONE WOLF adventures and others may be red herrings of no real use at all, so be selective in what you decide to keep.

There are many routes to the King, but only one involves a minimum of danger. With a wise choice of Kai Disciplines and a great deal of courage, any player should be able to complete the mission, no matter how weak their initial COMBAT SKILL or ENDURANCE points score.

The honour and memory of the Kai Lords will go with you on your perilous journey.

Good luck!

1

You must make haste for you sense it is not safe to linger by the smoking remains of the ruined monastery. The black-winged beasts could return at any moment. You must set out for the Sommerlund capital of Holmgard and tell the King the terrible news of the massacre: that the whole élite of Kai warriors, save yourself, have been slaughtered. Without the Kai Lords to lead her armies, Sommerlund will be at the mercy of their ancient enemy, the Darklords.

Fighting back tears, you bid farewell to your dead kinsmen. Silently, you promise that their deaths will be avenged. You turn away from the ruins and carefully descend the steep track.

At the foot of the hill, the path splits into two directions, both leading into a large wood.

> If you wish to take the right path into the wood, turn to **85**.
> If you wish to follow the left track, turn to **275**.
> If you wish to use your Kai Discipline of Sixth Sense, turn to **141**.

2

As you dash through the thickening trees, the shouts of the Giaks begin to fade behind you. You have nearly outdistanced them completely, when you crash headlong into a tangle of low branches.

Pick a number from the *Random Number Table*.

If you have picked a number *0–4*, turn to **343**.
If you have picked a number *5–9*, turn to **276**.

3

Staying close to the officer, you follow him through an arched portal and up a short flight of stairs to a long hall. Soldiers run back and forth bearing orders on ornate scrolls to officers stationed around the city wall.

A haggard and scar-faced man dressed in the white and purple robes of the King's court approaches you and bids you follow him to the citadel.

If you wish to follow this man, turn to **196**.
If you wish to decline his offer and return to the crowded streets, turn to **144**.

4

It is a small one-man canoe in very poor condition. The wood has split and warped, and the craft appears to be leaking in several places. You quickly patch up the worst of the holes with some clay and bail out the water. This seems to stop the leaking for the moment. Stowing your equipment at the bow, you set off downstream, using a piece of driftwood as a paddle.

After a short while, you hear the sound of horses galloping towards you along the left bank.

If you wish to hide in the bottom of the canoe, turn to **75**.

If you wish to try to attract their attention, turn to **175**.

If you wish to use the Kai Discipline of Sixth Sense, turn to **218**.

5

After about an hour of walking, the track slowly bears round to the east. You reach a shallow ford where a fast-flowing brook runs on a steep rocky course towards the south. Just beyond the ford is a junction where the track meets a wider path running north to south. Realizing that the north path will take you away from the capital, you turn right at the junction and head south.

Turn to **111**.

6

In the distance you can hear the sound of horses galloping nearer. You crouch behind a tree and wait as the riders come closer. They are the cavalry of the King's Guard wearing the white uniforms of His Majesty's army.

If you wish to call them, turn to **183**.

If you wish to let them pass and then continue on your way through the forest, turn to **200**.

7 – *Illustration I (overleaf)*

For what seems an eternity, the rush of the crowd carries you along like a leaf on a fast-flowing stream. You desperately fight to stay on your feet, but you feel weak and dizzy from your ordeal, and your legs

I.   From here you can see the magnificent view of the rooftops
and spires of Holmgard

are as heavy as lead. Suddenly, you catch a glimpse of a long, narrow stone stairway that leads up to the roof of an inn.

Gathering the last reserves of your strength, you dive for the stairs and climb slowly up to the top. From here you can see the magnificent view of the rooftops and spires of Holmgard, with the high stone walls of the citadel gleaming in the sun.

The houses and buildings of the capital are built very close to each other, and it is possible to jump from one roof to the next. In fact many of the citizens of Holmgard used to use the 'Roofways' (as they are known) when the heavy autumn rains made the unpaved parts of the streets too muddy for walking. But after many accidents, a royal decree forbade their use.

After careful thought, you decide to use the 'Roofways', as they are your only chance of reaching the King. You have hopped, skipped and jumped across several streets and you are only one street away from the citadel when you come to the end of a row of rooftops.

The jump to the next row is much further than anything you have tried before, and your stomach begins to feel as if it were full of butterflies. Determined to reach the citadel, you turn and take a long run-up to the jump. With blood pounding in your ears, you sprint to the edge of the roof and leap into space, your eyes fixed on the opposite rooftop.

Pick a number from the *Random Number Table*.

If you have picked a number that is *0–2*, turn to **108**.

(contd over)

If the number if *3–9*, turn to **25**.

8

Your Kai Sixth Sense warns there is a fierce battle raging in the south. Your common sense tells you that the south is also the quickest route to the capital.

Turn to **70** and choose your route.

9

You cannot move: you are being held rigid by some powerful force. Your eyes are drawn towards the mouth of the skeleton. From deep in the earth you hear a low humming, like the sound of millions of angry bees. A dull red glow appears in the empty eye sockets of the dead King and the humming increases until your ears are filled with the deafening roar. You are in the presence of an ancient evil, far older and stronger than the Darklords themselves.

If you possess a Vordak Gem, turn to **236**.
If you do not, turn to **292**.

10

You are sweating and your legs ache. In the middle distance you can see a group of cottages.

If you wish to enter a cottage and rest for a while, turn to **115**.
If you wish to press on, turn to **83**.

11

You quickly dodge into the doorway of a stable and hide your surgeon's cloak in the straw, for it would be better to be seen as a Kai Lord than as a charlatan.

Without wasting a second, you set off towards the Great Hall on the other side of the courtyard.

Turn to **139**.

12

The bodyguard looks at you with great suspicion and then slams the door shut. You can hear the sound of voices inside the caravan. Suddenly the door swings open and the face of a wealthy merchant appears.

He demands 10 Gold Crowns as payment for the ride.

If you have 10 Gold Crowns and wish to pay him, turn to **262**.

If you do not have enough Gold Crowns or do not wish to pay him, turn to **247**.

13

The path soon ends at a large clearing. In the centre of the clearing is a tree much taller and wider than any others you have seen in the forest.

Looking up through the massive branches you can see a large treehouse some twenty-five to thirty feet above the ground. There is no ladder, but the gnarled bark of the tree offers many footholds.

If you wish to climb the tree and search the tree-house, turn to **307**.

If you would rather press on, turn to **213**.

14

You reach the top of a small wooded hill on which several large boulders form a rough circle. Suddenly you hear a loud growl from behind a rock to your left.

If you wish to draw your weapon and prepare to fight, turn to **43**.

If you would rather take evasive action by running as fast as you can over the hill, turn to **106**.

15

You pass through a long, dark tunnel of overhanging branches that eventually opens out into a large clearing. On a stone plinth in the centre of the clearing is a Sword, sheathed in a black leather scabbard. A hand-written note has been tied to the hilt, but it is in a language which is foreign to you.

You may take the Sword if you wish, and note it on your *Action Chart*.

There are three exits from the clearing.

If you decide to go east, turn to **207**.

If you decide to go west, turn to **201**.

If you decide to go south, turn to **35**.

16

You manage to free a horse from the straps securing it to the caravan. It is frightened by the scent of the approaching Doomwolves, and the cries of their evil riders – the Giaks.

Preparing your weapon, you spur your skittish horse towards the oncoming beasts. They are less than fifty yards away and they are lowering their lances at you as they get nearer and nearer.

You are charging head-on towards each other. Turn to **192**.

17

You raise your weapon to strike at the beast as its razor-fanged mouth snaps shut just inches from your head. Buffeted by the beating of its wings you find it difficult to stand.

Deduct 1 point from your COMBAT SKILL and fight the Kraan.

Kraan: COMBAT SKILL 16   ENDURANCE 24

If you kill the creature, you quickly descend the far side of the hill to avoid the Giaks.

Pick a number from the *Random Number Table*.

If you pick *0*, turn to **53**.
If you pick *1–2*, turn to **274**.
If you pick *3–9*, turn to **331**.

18

You are awoken by the sound of troops in the distance. Across the lake you see the black-cloaked figures of Drakkarim and a pack of Doomwolves and their riders. A Kraan appears from above the trees and lands on the roof of the small wooden shack.

It is ridden by a creature dressed in red. The Kraan takes off and begins to fly across the lake to where you are hidden.

> If you wish to ride deeper in the forest, turn to **239**.
>
> If you wish to use the Kai Discipline of Camouflage, turn to **114**.
>
> If you wish to fight the creature, turn to **29**.

19

Just ahead through the tall trees you can see clumps of dark-red Gallowbrush, a thorny briar with sharp crimson barbs. The common name for this forest weed is 'Sleeptooth', for the thorns are very sharp and can make you feel weak and sleepy if they scratch your skin.

> You can avoid the Sleeptooth by returning to the track. Turn to **272**.
>
> Or you can push on through the briars, deeper into the forest, by turning to **119**.
>
> If you have the Kai Discipline of Tracking, turn to **69**.

20

It seems that whoever lived here left in a great hurry – and they must have left quite recently. A half-eaten meal still remains on the table, and a mug of dark Jala is still warm to the touch.

Searching a chest and small wardrobe, you find a Backpack, food (enough for two Meals), and a dagger.

If you wish to take these items, remember to mark them on your *Action Chart*. You continue your mission.

Turn to **272**.

21

You have ridden about two miles into the tangle of trees when the ground becomes very marshy.

Pick a number from the *Random Number Table*.

If it is below 5, your horse has suddenly plunged into thick mud up to its belly.

If the number is 5 or above, you manage to steer clear of the morass and may now turn to **189**.

If you are stuck, pick another number from the *Random Number Table*. If this time the number is 7 or less, the mud engulfs you up to your armpits. Your horse gives one last despairing scream as its muzzle disappears into the bubbling mud. If you scored above 7, you drag yourself on to firm ground and turn to **189**.

If not, then this is your last chance! If you pick any number except a 9, the foul-smelling bog sucks you under and claims another victim. Your life and your mission end here.

But if you have picked a 9, turn to **312**.

22

Knocking aside the leader, you sprint off along the highway. Then behind you the ominous click of a crossbow being cocked sends a shiver down your spine.

Pick a number from the *Random Number Table*.

If you have picked a number *0–4* turn to **181**.
If you have picked a number *5–9*, turn to **145**.

23 – *Illustration II*

The corridor soon widens into a large hall. At the far end, a stone staircase leads up to a huge door. Two black candles on either side of the stone steps dimly illuminate the chamber. You notice that no wax has melted, and as you get nearer you can feel that they give off no heat. Ancient engravings cover the stone surfaces of the walls.

Anxious to leave this evil tomb, you examine the door for a latch. An ornate pin appears to lock the door, but there is also a keyhole in the lockplate.

If you wish to remove the pin, turn to **337**.
If you have the Kai Discipline of Mind Over Matter, turn to **151**.
If you have a Golden Key, turn to **326**.

24

The merchant shouts to the driver of the caravan to jump. 'We're under attack!' he cries, disappearing through a circular window.

If you decide to jump after him, turn to **234**.
If you decide to run through the caravan and grab the reins of the horse team, turn to **184**.

25

You land with such a crash on the opposite roof, that the wind is knocked out of you and you lie flat on your back with your head in a spin.

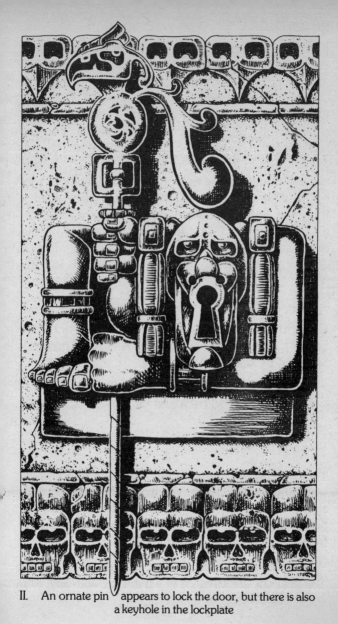

II.   An ornate pin   appears to lock the door, but there is also
      a keyhole in the lockplate

It takes a minute or so for you to realize that you've made it and are perfectly safe. When you are sure you are all right, you jump up and let out a shout for joy at your skill and daring.

Quickly you find a way across the roof and climb down a long drainpipe to the street below. You see the large iron doors of the citadel open, and a wagon drawn by two large horses tries to leave. The horses are frightened by the noisy crowd and they both rear up, causing the wagon to smash a front wheel against the door. In the confusion, you see a chance to enter and quickly slip inside just as the guards slam the doors shut.

Turn to **139**.

26

Cautiously, you move along the corridor until you come to a sharp eastward turn. A strange greenish light can be seen in the distance.

If you wish to continue, turn to **249**.
If you wish to go back and try the southern route, turn to **100**.

27

You walk along this path for over an hour, carefully watching the sky above you in case the Kraan attack again. Up ahead, a large tree has fallen across the path. As you approach, you can hear voices coming from the other side of the massive trunk.

If you choose to attack, turn to **250**.
If you choose to listen to what the voices say, turn to **52**.

28

After a few hundred yards, the path joins another one running north to south.

If you wish to go northwards, turn to **130**.
If you wish to head south, turn to **147**.

29

You stride out to the water's edge and prepare yourself for combat. The Kraan and its rider spot you and begin to speed across the lake barely inches above the surface.

The rider lets out a scream that freezes your blood. He is a Vordak, a fierce lieutenant of the Darklords.

He is upon you and you must fight him. Deduct 2 points from your COMBAT SKILL unless you have the Kai Discipline of Mindshield, for the creature is attacking you with its Mindforce as well as with a huge black mace.

Vordak: COMBAT SKILL 17   ENDURANCE 25

If you win the fight, turn to **270**.

30

The people look tired and hungry. They have come many miles from their burning city. Suddenly, you hear the beat of huge wings coming from the north.

'Kraan, Kraan! Hide yourselves!' the cry goes up all along the road.

Just in front of you, a wagon carrying small children breaks down, its right wheel jammed in a furrow. The children scream in panic.

(contd over)

If you wish to help the children, turn to **194**.
If you'd rather run for the cover of the trees, turn to **261**.

31

You try to comfort the injured man as best you can, but his wounds are serious and he is soon unconscious again. Covering him with his cape, you turn and press deeper into the forest.

Turn to **264**.

32

You have ridden about three miles when, in the distance, you spot the unmistakeable silhouette of five large Doomwolves. Riding on their backs are Giaks. They seem to be going on ahead to where the path leads down into an open meadow. Suddenly, one of the Giaks leaves the others and begins to ride back along the path towards you.

If you wish to hide in the undergrowth and let him pass, turn to **176**.
If you wish to fight him, turn to **340**.

33

The floor of the cave is quite dry and dusty. As you explore deeper in the half-light, you detect the stale odour of rotting flesh. Littering a crevice are the bones, fur and teeth of several small animals. You notice a small cloth bag among these remains which you open to discover 3 Gold Crowns. Pocketing these coins, you leave what appears to be the lair of a mountain cat and carefully descend the hill.

Turn to **248**.

34 – *Illustration III (overleaf)*

Without warning, a terrible apparition in red robes swoops down from the sky on the back of a Kraan. Its cry freezes your blood. The beast is a Vordak, a fierce lieutenant of the Darklords.

He is above you and you must fight him.

Deduct 2 points from your COMBAT SKILL unless you have the Kai Discipline of Mindshield, for the creature is attacking you with the power of its Mindforce as well as with a huge black mace.

Vordak: COMBAT SKILL 17   ENDURANCE 25

If you win, turn to **328**.

35

The forest is becoming denser, and the path more tangled with thorny briars. Almost completely hidden by the undergrowth, you notice another path branching off towards the east. Your current route seems to be coming to a prickly end, so you decide to follow the new path eastwards.

Turn to **207**.

III.   A terrible apparition in red robes swoops down from the sky on the back of a Kraan

36

The old watchtower ladder is rotten and several rungs break as you climb. Pick a number from the *Random Number Table*.

If the number is 4 or lower you have fallen, lose 2 ENDURANCE points and turn to **140**.

If the number is 5 or higher, you do not fall. Turn to **323**.

37

You are feeling tired and hungry and you must stop to eat. After your Meal, you retrace your steps back to the citadel and begin to walk around the high, indomitable stone wall.

You discover another entrance on the eastern side, guarded as before by two armoured soldiers.

If you wish to approach them and tell your story, turn to **289**.

If you wish to use the Kai Discipline of Camouflage, turn to **282**.

38

For half an hour or more you press on through the forest, through the rich vegetation and ferns. You happen upon a small clear stream where you stop for a few minutes to wash your face and drink of the cold, fresh water.

Feeling revitalized, you cross the stream and press on. You soon notice the smell of woodsmoke which seems to be drifting towards you from the north.

If you wish to investigate the smell of woodsmoke, turn to **128**.

(contd over)

If you would rather avoid the source of this smoke, turn to **347**.

39

After a few seconds, two small furry faces nervously appear over the top of the trunk. They say they are Kakarmi and tell you that the Kraan are everywhere. To the west lie the remains of their village but little is left of it now. They are trying to find the rest of their tribe who took to the forest when the 'Black-wings' attacked. They point behind them – east along the path – and tell you that the trail appears to be a dead end, but that if you continue through the undergrowth for a few yards more, you will find a watchtower where the path splits into three directions. Take the east path. This leads to the King's highway between the capital city – Holmgard – and the northern port of Toran.

You thank the Kakarmi, and bid them farewell.

Turn to **228**.

40

Keeping a careful watch on the huts for any sign of the enemy, you make your way around the clearing under the cover of the trees and bracken. Rejoining the track, you hurry away from Fogwood.

Turn to **105**.

41 – *Illustration IV*

Three rangers gallop past the river bank, closely followed by the Giaks on their snarling Doomwolves.

The bank is steep and you are spotted by the Giak leader who orders five of his troops to open fire at you

IV.   The Giak leader orders five of his troops to open fire at you with their bows with their bows. Their black arrows rain down on you.

> If you decide to paddle downstream as fast as you can, turn to **174**.
>
> If you decide to head for the cover of the trees on the opposite bank, turn to **116**.

42

You follow the track for nearly an hour when you come to a crossroads.

> If you wish to continue east, turn to **86**.
>
> If you would rather head north, turn to **238**.
>
> If you decide to venture south, turn to **157**.
>
> Or if you prefer to go west, turn to **147**.

43

From behind the rock a huge black bear comes into view. It advances slowly towards you, its mouth open and its face lined in anger and pain.

You notice that it is badly wounded and is bleeding from its neck and back. You must fight it.

Black Bear: COMBAT SKILL 16   ENDURANCE 10

> If you win, turn to **195**.
>
> After three rounds of combat, you position yourself so that you can run down the hill. If you wish to evade at this time then turn to **106** and chance being wounded as you flee.

44

Without warning, the old track ends abruptly at the edge of a steep slope. The ground here is very loose and unstable. You lose your footing and fall headlong over the edge.

Pick a number from the *Random Number Table*.

If you have picked a number that is 0–4, turn to **277**.

If the number is 5–9, turn to **338**.

45

These men are not what they seem. The tunic of the leader is genuine but it is heavily bloodstained around the collar, as if its true owner had been murdered. Their weapons are not army issue, but expensive and lavishly decorated like the weapons made by the armourers of Durenor.

The leader has a crossbow slung over his pack. An attempt to run would be suicide. You decide that you must fight them or you will surely be murdered as soon as you drop your weapon.

Turn to **180**.

46

You have covered about two miles when the trees ahead thin out. You can see a small wooden shack on the edge of a lake. A cloaked man approaches you and offers to row you and your horse across the lake for a fee of 2 Gold Crowns.

If you accept the offer, turn to **246**.

If you refuse and try to ride around the lake, turn to **90**.

If you have the Kai Discipline of Sixth Sense, turn to **296**.

47

Breathless and sweating, you claw your way towards the summit of the hill. Suddenly, a large winged shadow passes across the hillside. You look up to see a Kraan circling the peak above. Behind you the Giaks are gaining ground.

Do you stand and fight the Giaks where you are, using the high ground to your advantage? If so, turn to **136**.

Or do you grit your teeth and press on towards the peak of the hill? Turn to **322**.

48

Your Sixth Sense warns you that these troops are not all they seem. You can detect an aura of evil about them. They are in the service of the Darklords.

You must leave here quickly before you are spotted. Turn to **243**.

49

As you begin to read the inscription, you notice a shadow moving towards you from behind the screen.

Pick a number from the *Random Number Table*.

If you have chosen a number that is 0–4, turn to **339**.

If the number is 5–9, turn to **60**.

50

The sound of fighting can be heard in the distance.

If you wish to continue towards the sound of battle, turn to **97**.

If you wish to avoid the fighting, change direction and turn to **243**.

51 – *Illustration V (overleaf)*

You climb the wooded bank of the river and see the log walls of the fieldworks disappearing into the distance.

A battle rages about two miles away and the log wall has collapsed in several places where the Darklords are attacking.

Most of the fieldworks ahead are unmanned, the soldiers having left to supply reinforcements for the raging battle.

> There is a gate in the log wall. If you wish to approach it, turn to **288**.
> If you would prefer to climb over the wall instead, turn to **221**.

52

Now that you are closer, you can make out that the voices are not human. The sound is more like a kind of grunting and squeaking.

> If you have the Kai Discipline of Animal Kinship, turn to **225**.
> If not, you must climb over the tree and face whatever lurks on the other side. Turn to **250**.

53

A searing pain tears through your right leg as it is twisted and crushed by the weight of your body. Down and down you tumble, until you finally land in a ditch at the base of the hill with such force that the

V.   The log wall has collapsed in several   places where
     the Darklords are attacking

wind is knocked out of you and you lose consciousness.

You are awoken by the sharp pain of something stabbing your chest. It proves to be the tip of a Giak spear. You are greeted by the malicious sneer of its owner as he pins your left arm to the ground. Instinctively you reach for your weapon but it is no longer there.

Defenceless against the cruel Giaks, the last thing that you see before all light fades is the jagged point of a Giak lance hurtling down towards your throat.

Your mission ends here.

54

It would seem that the heavens have not heard your prayers. A spear whistles past your head and embeds itself in the neck of your galloping horse. With a shriek of pain, the horse topples forward and you both roll in a tangled heap on the highway.

Dazed and pinned down by the weight of the dead body of your horse, the last thing you remember are the sharp penetrating spearheads of the Giak lances.

You have failed in your mission.

55

Just as the Giak makes his leap, you race forward and strike out with your weapon – knocking the creature away from the young wizard's back.

You jump onto the struggling Giak and strike again. Due to the surprise of your attack, add 4 points to your COMBAT SKILL for the duration of this fight but remember to deduct it again as soon as the fight is over.

Giak: COMBAT SKILL 9   ENDURANCE 9

If you win, turn to **325**.

56

You hear the scream of a large winged beast above the trees. It is a Kraan, a deadly servant of the Darklords. Quickly you hide beneath the thick fronds of fern until the horrible shrieks have passed away.

Now turn to **222**.

57

The cabin has only one room. In it you see a wooden table and two benches, a large bed made of straw bales lashed together, several bottles of coloured liquids and an embroidered rug in the centre of the floor.

If you choose to take a closer look at the bottles, turn to **164**.

If you choose to pull back the rug, turn to **109**.

If you choose to leave the room and investigate the stable, turn to **308**.

58

Bracing yourself for the run, you head off down the ridge at a steady pace. To the west, the army of the Darklords looks like a giant pot of black ink that has been spilled between the mountains and is spreading into the land below.

You have been running for twenty minutes when you catch sight of a pack of Doomwolves lining a shallow ridge to your right.

> If you decide to flatten yourself against the rocks along the side of the road and wait until they pass, turn to **286**.
> If you decide to carry on running, but draw your weapon just in case they attack, turn to **160**.

59

Peering into the darkness, you notice that rough stairs have been cut into the earth and that the mouth of the cave is in fact the entrance to a tunnel.

Carefully descending the slippery stairway, you notice a small silver box on a shelf at the bottom of the staircase.

> If you want to open the silver box, turn to **124**.
> If you wish to return to the surface and press on, turn to **106**.
> If you wish to investigate the tunnel further, turn to **211**.

60

The last thing you remember before darkness engulfs you is the flash of a long curved steel knife. You have become yet another victim of the Sage and his robber son – the very one who has just slit your throat!

(contd over)

Your quest ends here.

61

At last you can reach the wooden fieldworks surrounding the outer city. As you race towards a sentry post, you can hear the excited shouts of the guards cheering you on. Thank the gods that they recognize you, for you must appear a ragged and suspicious figure. Your cloak is torn and hangs in tatters, your face is scratched and blood-smeared and the dust of the Graveyard covers you from head to toe.

Splashing through a shallow stream, you stagger towards the gate. The full horror of the Graveyard encounter begins to catch up with you. The last thing you recall before exhaustion robs you of consciousness, is falling into the outstretched arms of two soldiers who have run from the fieldworks to help you.

Turn to **268**.

62

The 'soldiers' lie dead at your feet. They were bandits who were stealing from the refugees of Toran, and from the abandoned houses and farms in the area.

Searching their bodies you find 28 Gold Crowns and two Backpacks containing enough food for 3 Meals. They had been armed with a crossbow and three Swords. The crossbow had been damaged in the fight, but the Swords are untouched and you may keep one if you wish.

You adjust your equipment, give a cautious glance towards the west and continue your run towards the outer defences of the capital.

Turn to **288**.

63 – *Illustration VI (overleaf)*

The wild old man is screaming at you. He blames you for the war and curses the Kai Lords as agents of the Darklords. He will not listen to reason and you must fight him.

Madman: COMBAT SKILL 11   ENDURANCE 10

If you win, turn to **269**.

64

You are awoken by the cries of a Kraan circling above the caravan. It is early morning and the sky is clear and bright. You can see a pack of Doomwolves less than a quarter of a mile away along the highway ahead. They are preparing to attack. You must act quickly.

If you decide to gather your equipment and run for the cover of the trees, turn to **188**.

If you decide to cut free one of the horses and try to break through the attacking Doomwolves to the clear road beyond, then turn to **16**.

65

Your senses scream at you that this place is very evil. Leave as quickly as you can.

Turn to **104**.

VI.   The wild old man is screaming at you

66

Startled, you turn around to see a burly sergeant and two soldiers running towards you, their swords drawn as if to strike.

You prepare to defend yourself for it looks as if they are about to attack first and ask questions later; but suddenly the sergeant calls his men to a halt. He has recognized your cloak. They put away their weapons and apologize many times for their mistake. The sergeant orders one of the men to fetch the captain of the Guard as he leads you to the doors of the Great Hall.

You are greeted by a tall and handsome warrior who listens intently to your story. When you have finished the account of your perilous journey to the capital, you notice a tear in the brave man's eye as he bids you to follow him. You walk through the splendid halls and corridors of the inner Palace. The richness and grandeur are a wonder to behold. You eventually arrive at a large carved door, guarded by two soldiers wearing silver armour.

You are about to meet the King.

Turn to **350**.

67

Your Kai Discipline of Tracking reveals to you fresh paw prints leading off along the south path.

They are the prints of a black bear, an animal renowned for its ferocity. You decide the east path would be a much safer route.

Turn to **140**.

68

After a short walk, you reach a junction where a path crosses your present route heading from west to east.

If you wish to turn west, go to **130**.

If you wish to head east, turn to **15**.

69

You are very near a friendly village.

Avoid the Gallowbrush and turn to **272**.

70

You have reached a small bridge. A track follows the stream towards the east. A much narrower path disappears into thick forest towards the south.

If you wish to go east, turn to **28**.
If you wish to go south, turn to **157**.
If you wish to use the Kai Discipline of Sixth Sense, turn to **8**.

71

You are winded but not hurt. You have fallen fifteen feet or so through the roof of an underground tomb. The walls are sheer and you cannot climb them. An arched tunnel leads out of the tomb towards the east, in front of which lies the sarcophagus of some ancient noble.

If you wish to open the sarcophagus to see if it contains any treasure, turn to **242**.

If you wish to leave via the tunnel, turn to **104**.

If you wish to use the Kai Discipline of Sixth Sense, turn to **65**.

72

You turn to face a sneering Giak and the razor-fanged jaws of its mount. You must fight them as one enemy.

Giak + Doomwolf: COMBAT SKILL 15   ENDURANCE 24

If you win, turn to **265**.

73

Pulling your green cloak about you, you blend into the foliage and rocks. Peering carefully up at the track, you are shocked to see that they are not the King's men at all.

They are Drakkarim, some of the Darklords cruellest troops. They must have disguised themselves as soldiers of the King in order to get this far into the forest. Thanking your Kai training for saving your life, you silently slip away from the stream and push on into the forest.

Turn to **243**.

74

The Kraan and its riders land on the track barely ten feet from where you are hidden.

The Giaks leap from the scaly backs of the Kraan and move towards you, their spears raised to strike. You have been seen.

If you decide to fight them, turn to **138**.

If you decide to run deeper into the forest without delay, turn to **281**.

75

Peering out carefully, you can see three green-clad men on horses racing along the bank. You recognize them as border rangers, the regiment of the King's Army that police the western borders. One of them is wounded and is slumped over the neck of his horse.

Close behind follow a pack of twenty Doomwolves. Their Giak riders are firing arrows at the rangers which fall all around them. One ranger drops from his horse and rolls down the river bank, a black arrow deeply embedded in his right leg.

If you wish to help the ranger, turn to **260**.

If you wish to stay hidden and drift downstream, turn to **163**.

76

The Gem feels very hot and burns your hand. Lose 2 ENDURANCE points. You quickly grab it with the edge of your cloak and slip it into the pocket of your jacket. A Gem that size must be worth hundreds of Crowns!

You smile at your good fortune, mount your horse and ride off along the south track.

Turn to **118**.

77

The Mountain Giaks are unaccustomed to pursuing their prey through forests and you soon outdistance them, until finally the sound of their grunts and curses disappears completely.

When you are satisfied that they have given up the chase, you stop for a few minutes to catch your breath and check your equipment. With the memory of your ruined monastery still blazing in your mind, you gather up your meagre belongings and push on.

Turn to **19**.

78

As the caravan careers past, you leap for the tailboard and manage to hold fast. Pulling yourself upright, you find that you are standing on the bottom rung of a ladder leading to the rear door of the wagon. Suddenly the top half of the door flies open and you are confronted by the angry face of a bodyguard.

(contd over)

If you decide to inform him that you are a Kai Lord
with an urgent message for the King, turn to
132.

If you decide to offer him Gold Crowns for safe
passage to the capital, turn to **12**.

If you decide to attack the guard with your
weapon, turn to **220**.

79

You come to a small footbridge across a fast-flowing
stream. On the other side of the bridge the path turns
south. You cross the bridge and follow the path.

Turn to **204**.

80

You stumble backwards through the front door,
clutching your burnt chest with both hands. Smoke is
billowing from the shop and you must run – before
the Sage or his robber son catch you.

You make it back to the main street and lose yourself
in the rush of the crowds.

Turn to **7**.

81

After nearly an hour, the Kraan and their cruel riders
vanish towards the west. As the shocked refugees
start to emerge from the woods, you can hear the
sound of horses in the distance galloping nearer. You
stay hidden and wait as the riders come closer. They
are the cavalry of the King's Guard wearing the white
uniforms of His Majesty's army.

If you wish to call to them, turn to **183**.

If you would rather continue along the forest edge towards the south, turn to **200**.

82

The giant Gourgaz lies dead at your feet. His evil followers hiss at you and then fall back from the bridge. The Prince's soldiers form a protective wall around you and their dying leader with their shields. Black arrows whistle past your head.

The dying Prince looks up into your eyes and says, 'Kai Lord, you must take a message to my father. The enemy is too strong, we cannot hold him. The King must seek that which is in Durenor or all is lost. Take my horse and ride for the capital. May the luck of the gods ride with you.'

You bid a sad farewell to the Prince, mount his white steed and head south along the forest path. The battle still rages behind you as the Prince's men fight off another assault on the bridge.

Turn to **235**.

83

You have run about a mile when three soldiers appear from beneath a small footbridge. They demand that you halt and drop your weapons and equipment.

They are bloodstained and unshaven. Their leader is wearing the tunic of a soldier of the Toran garrison.

If you wish to do as they say, turn to **205**.

If you wish to prepare to fight them, turn to **180**.

If you demand to know what they want, turn to **232**.

If you posses the Kai Discipline of Sixth Sense, turn to **45**.

84

Just as you feel the air beating on your back, you slip free of your horse and roll over – landing with a splash in a muddy ditch by the side of the highway.

You are uninjured, and you quickly scramble to your feet and make a dash for the cover of the trees – but with thirty yards left to run, you see the Kraan circling above for another dive.

Turn to **188**.

85

The path is wide and leads straight into thick undergrowth. The trees are tall here and unusually quiet. You walk for over a mile when suddenly you hear the beating of large wings directly above you. Looking up, you are shocked to see the sinister black outline of a Kraan diving to attack you.

If you draw your weapon and prepare to fight, turn to **229**.

If you evade the attack by running south, deeper into the forest, turn to **99**.

86

You soon reach another crossroads.

If you wish to journey east, turn to **6**.
If you wish to head north, turn to **35**.
If you prefer to go south, turn to **167**.
Or if you wish to turn west, turn to **42**.

87

Focusing your powers on the lock, you try to visualize the inner mechanism. Gradually its image appears in your mind's eye. It is old and corroded but it still functions. You are in danger of losing your concentration when a subtle click confirms that your effort has not been in vain.

The pin is an easier task. Slowly it rises out of the lock and falls to the floor. The granite door swings towards you on hidden hinges and the grey half-light of the Graveyard floods into the tomb. The exit is overgrown with Graveweed and you suffer many small cuts to your face and hands as you fight your way through to the surface. You are startled by a sudden noise. You turn to see the disembodied head of a corpse laughing at you.

In blind panic, you race through the eerie necropolis towards the southern gate.

Turn to **61**.

88

You cautiously peer around the rock to see a soldier lying on his back. By his side is a Spear and shield. On the shield is the painting of a white pegasus – the Prince of Sommerlund's emblem. He is one of the Prince's soldiers, and he is only just conscious. His uniform is badly torn, and you can see that he has a deep wound in his left arm. As you move nearer, his eyes flicker open. 'Heal me, my Lord,' he begs. 'I can barely feel my arm.'

If you possess and wish to use the Kai Discipline of Healing on this man, turn to **216**.

If you do not possess the skill, or do not want to use it, then turn to **31**.

89

In a cloud of dust and loose rocks you career down the steep hillside. The Kraan is still circling above as if waiting to direct the Giaks after you.

Pick a number from the *Random Number Table*.

If you have picked *0–1*, turn to **53**.
If it is *2–4*, turn to **274**.
It it is *5–9*, turn to **316**.

90

Night falls and you are soon engulfed in total darkness. To press on would be useless, for you would be sure to lose your way. Tethering your horse to a tree, you pull your green Kai cloak about you and fall into a restless sleep.

Turn to **18**.

91

The small shop is dark and musty. Books and bottles of every size and colour fill the many shelves. As you close the door, a small black dog begins to yap at you. A bald man appears from behind a large screen and bids you welcome. He politely enquires as to the nature of your visit and offers you a choice of his wares from the glass counter.

If you wish to look at his wares, turn to **152**.

If you would rather decline his offer and return to the street, turn to **7**.

If you have the Kai Discipline of Sixth Sense, turn to **198**.

92

You dive for cover not a moment too soon, for a hail of black arrows scream out of the woods and bombard the area where you were standing seconds before. Pulling your cloak around you to blend into the dense bracken, you dash through the forest and away from the hidden ambushers as fast as possible. This entire area is infested by Giaks and you must escape as quickly as you can. You run without rest for over an hour until you happen to fall upon a straight forest path heading towards the east. You follow the path, taking care to keep watch for signs of the enemy.

Turn to **13**.

93

You turn and run for the stairs just as a large block falls with a crash behind you. The room you were in has been completely sealed off. As you escape into the daylight, you glimpse behind you the crooked figure of an old druid as he raises his staff. A second later, a bolt of lightning explodes at your feet. You do not stop but run headlong down the hill, cursing the delay but thankful for your Sixth Sense.

Turn to **106**.

94

The Sage, seeing that you have killed his son, turns and runs from the shop by a back door.

You find 12 Gold Crowns in the robber's purse and another 4 Gold Crowns in a wooden box under the counter. Carefully examining the potions and the wand you soon realize that they are all cheap counterfeits. In fact the entire shop is full of imitations. You shake your head and return to the main street.

Turn to **7**.

95

You soon stumble upon a narrow forest track running from north to south.

If you wish to set off along the track towards the north, turn to **240**.

If you wish to go south instead, turn to **5**.

96

Holding your breath, you tighten your grip on your weapon and prepare to strike. The tension is unbearable – the Giaks are so close that the foul stench of their unwashed bodies fills your nostrils. You hear them curse in their strange alien tongue and then leave the ledge and start to scramble towards the peak. When you are sure they have gone, you finally exhale and wipe the sweat from your eyes.

If you wish to explore the cave further, turn to **33**.
If you wish to leave the cave and descend the hill in case the Giaks return, turn to **248**.

97 – *Illustration VII (overleaf)*

Ahead of you, you can see a fierce battle raging across a stone bridge. The clash of steel and the cries of men and beasts echo through the forest. In the midst of the fighting, you see Prince Pelathar, the King's son. He is in combat with a large grey Gourgaz who is wielding a black axe above his scaly head. Suddenly, the Prince falls wounded – a black arrow in his side.

If you wish to defend the fallen Prince, turn to **255**.
If you wish to run into the forest, turn to **306**.

98

The guards seem to believe your story and bow with respect to your rank of Kai Lord. One of them pulls a concealed bell-rope and the huge doors start to swing open. They usher you inside and you hear the doors close behind you.

Turn to **139**.

VII. The clash of steel and the cries of men and beasts echo
through the forest

99

You dive into the undergrowth just as the beast screams past your head. You quickly look back to see the Kraan turning in the air in preparation for another dive. You scramble to your feet and run deeper into the safety of the forest.

Turn to **222**.

100

The cold corridor suddenly makes an abrupt turning towards the east. You notice a greenish glow that lights the tunnel in the far distance. As you creep nearer you can see that the corridor opens out into a larger chamber.

The strange light seems to emanate from a large bowl resting upon the top of a granite throne. On a plinth in front of the throne stands a statue. It looks like a winged serpent curved in the shape of an 'S'.

If you wish to sit on the throne, turn to **161**.
If you wish to examine the statue, turn to **133**.
If you wish to look for an exit from this chamber, turn to **257**.

101

The noise of battle soon fades behind you but the ensuing silence is broken by a voice in your head that accuses you of being a coward, and deserting a fellow human in danger. You try to rid yourself of your nagging conscience by telling yourself that your mission is far more important, and that not only is the life of the young magician in peril but the lives of all your countrymen depend on you reaching the capital alive.

Suddenly, the sight of a Giak war party in the distance makes you quickly take cover and hide. But it is too late – they have spotted you and you must run as fast as you can.

Turn to **281**.

102

As you descend the rocky slope towards the Graveyard of the Ancients, you are aware of a strange mist and cloud that swirls all around this grey and forbidding place, blocking the sun and covering the Graveyard in a perpetual gloom. A chill creeps forward to greet your approach.

With a feeling of deep dread, you enter the eerie necropolis.

Turn to **284**.

103

The overgrown path leads to a junction where another track branches off towards the east.

If you wish to take this path, turn to **13**.
If you would rather continue towards the northeast, turn to **287**.

104

The walls are dank and slimy. The stale air chokes you and cobwebs brush across your face. You can feel panic grip your stomach, as the tunnel gets darker and darker.

You reach a junction where the tunnel meets a corridor leading from north to south.

If you wish to turn north, go to **26**.
If you wish to go south, turn to **100**.

105

In the distance, perched on the branch of an old oak tree is a jet black raven.

If you have the Kai Discipline of Animal Kinship, you may call to this bird by turning to **298**.
If you do not possess this skill, turn to **335**.

106

Eventually you come to the edge of a fast-flowing icy stream. The white water cascades over the mossy rocks and disappears towards the east.

If you wish to follow the stream to the east, turn to **263**.

If you would rather explore upstream, turn to **334**.

107

Running across the room, you lash out at the skulls, smashing them to fragments. You notice that inside each skull is a bubbling grey jelly that seems to writhe and change its shape, sprouting bat-like wings and suckers from its glistening form. In horror and loathing, you race for the exit corridor and escape just as a heavy portcullis falls with a crash, completely sealing off the chamber.

Turn to **23**.

108

You fly in an arc through the air towards the opposite roof. Everything seems to be happening in slow motion. You see the teeming crowds below in the street, and a nest of callysparrows in the eaves of a roof to your right. You hear their startled cries as you land with a crash on the other side. But it is the last sound that you will ever hear. The tiles splinter and collapse and you fall through the four floors of the 'Green Slipper Inn' breaking your back in several places.

Your mission and your life end here.

109

The only thing under the carpet is dirt!

You may take a closer look at the bottles by turning to **164**.

Or you can leave the room and investigate the stable by turning to **308**.

110

You quickly take aim and hurl the rock at the Giak's head as hard as you can, but to your horror the creature ducks and the rock arcs harmlessly over its back. You must act immediately to save the wizard.

Turn to **55**.

111

Only a few minutes after leaving the junction, you see in the distance a small log cabin and stable. On arrival you check the interior through a side window. The cabin looks deserted.

If you wish to enter the cabin, turn to **57**.

If you wish to search the stable, turn to **308**.

112

Suddenly, the large rock you are hiding behind is rolled aside and you are faced by two snarling Giaks intent on your death. The cavemouth is a narrow entrance and you can only fight the Giaks one at a time.

Giak 1: COMBAT SKILL 13   ENDURANCE 10
Giak 2: COMBAT SKILL 12   ENDURANCE 10

If you win, you may explore the cave further by turning to **33**.

Or you may leave and descend the hill. Turn to **248**.

113

You have been walking for over half an hour when your eye is caught by some bright red flowers growing near to a mossy bank. You recognize the plants to be Laumspur, a rare and beautiful herb much prized for its healing properties.

Kneeling down, you pick a handful of Laumspur and place it in your Backpack. You may eat this herb to regain lost ENDURANCE points. Each Meal of Laumspur will restore 3 ENDURANCE points, and you have gathered enough for two such Meals. Closing your pack, you continue your mission.

If you wish to head northeast, turn to **347**.
If you wish to head east, turn to **295**.

114

You coax the horse to lie down and begin to cover him and yourself with branches and dead leaves. You hear the wings of the Kraan as it passes over the trees. It returns and circles above you, but soon retreats back across the lake.

You decide to leave now, in case it returns with some of its friends.

Turn to **239**.

115

You stumble into the first building and fall to the floor exhausted. You can smell cooked meat. You notice a small cauldron hanging over the embers of a dying fire, and a large oak table that has been set for a meal. Whoever lived here must have left in a great hurry this very morning. There is water in a jug and a loaf of fresh bread on the table.

If you decide to take a quick Meal, turn to **150**.
If you decide to search the building, turn to **177**.
If you would rather leave now and continue your
    run, turn to **83**.

116

As you climb out of the muddy water, black arrows fall all around you. Quickly, you dash for the cover of the trees and wait for the Giaks to leave the opposite bank, before continuing on foot towards the capital.

Turn to **321**.

117

The man is badly injured and near to death. If you have the Kai Discipline of Healing, you may ease the pain of his wounds but he has been so seriously hurt he is beyond repair by your skills alone. He soon lapses into unconsciousness. You try to make him as comfortable as possible beneath a large forest oak, before leaving and pressing on through the thick woodland towards the northeast.

Turn to **330**.

118

You spur your horse to a gallop and race down the long straight path. In the far distance you can just make out the silhouette of Holmgard on the horizon, its high walls and tall spires glinting in the morning sun. Your path joins a highway running from north to south. It is the main turnpike road between the northern port of Toran and the capital. You set off twards Holmgard,your eyes peeled for Kraan in the clear morning sky.

Turn to **224**.

119

The Gallowbrush tears your cloak and scratches deep into your arms and legs as you slowly force your way through. Fifteen minutes later you emerge from the briars and stagger onwards between the trees.

Deduct 2 ENDURANCE points from your current score for the wounds you have sustained.

You feel a little dizzy as you push on, and your eyelids seem very heavy. You suddenly find yourself at the edge of a steep wooded slope.

If you wish to slide down the slope as carefully as you can, turn to **226**.

If you do not feel that you are up to the risk of this tricky descent in your present sleepy state, walk around the edge of the ridge by turning to **38**.

120

Behind you can hear the blood-crazy Giaks killing the caravan horses. You risk a quick glance over your shoulder and see a Kraan start to climb high into the air. Will it attack you or is it interested in something else? The dark shadow that is gradually getting larger all around you tells you that *you* are its intended victim. The Kraan is diving full speed at you!

If you wait until it is about to strike, then jump from the saddle, turn to **84**.

If you head as fast as you can for the trees, turn to **171**.

If you put your head down, pray to the heavens for good luck and gallop on regardless, turn to **54**.

121 – *Illustration VIII (overleaf)*

After a few minutes walking you see a stranger, clad in red, standing in the centre of the track ahead. He has his back towards you, and his head is covered by the hood of his robes. Perched on his outstretched arm is the black raven that you saw earlier.

If you wish to call the stranger, turn to **342**.

If you wish to approach the stranger cautiously, turn to **309**.

If you would rather draw your weapon and attack, turn to **283**.

122

Immediately the horse senses your communication, he calms down. You walk towards the beautiful animal and stroke his head reassuringly. You sense that he is frightened and confused. Mounting him,

VIII.   Perched on his outstretched arm is the black raven that
you saw earlier

you lead him off to the path and head south once again.

Turn to **206**.

123

As the creature dies, its body slowly dissolves into a vile green liquid. You notice that all of the grass and the plants beneath the smoking fluid are beginning to shrivel and die. A large valuable looking Gem lies on the ground near to the decaying body.

Further along the track you can see a large war party of Giaks running towards you.

If you wish to take the Gem, turn to **304**.
If you would rather leave it and run, turn to **2**.

124

Inside the box you find 15 Gold Crowns and a Silver Key. If you wish to keep the key, remember to mark it on your *Action Chart*.

You can continue to investigate the tunnel by turning to **211**.
Of you may leave and descend the hill by turning to **106**.

125

The path opens out into a large clearing. You notice strange claw prints in the earth. Kraan have landed here. By the number of prints and by the size of the area disturbed, you judge that at least five of the foul creatures landed here in the last twelve hours.

You see two exits on the far side of the clearing. One leads west, the other south.

(contd over)

If you wish to take the south path, turn to **27**.

If you wish to take the west path, turn to **214**.

If you have the Kai Discipline of Tracking, turn to **301**.

126

You ride deeper and deeper into the forest. Silently you thank the Prince for such a fine horse, for although the ground is a tangle of briars and roots, he never once falters. The Doomwolves are soon left far behind and you bring your horse to a halt. The light has faded fast and it is almost night.

If you wish to press on ahead, turn to **46**.

If you wish to bear left (the same direction as the path you left far behind) then turn to **143**.

127

After an hour of marching, the Drakkarim suddenly halt as a large, grey scaly creature approaches along the track. As the beast draws closer, you can smell its fetid breath on your face. It lets out a roar and grabs your head in its powerful webbed hands. The last thing you hear is the sharp crack of your spine snapping.

Your quest ends here.

128

Carefully parting the dense foliage, you are horrified by the sight that meets you. In a small clearing ahead, three Giaks have tied a man to a wooden stake and are setting fire to a mass of brushwood bundled at his feet. You recognize his tunic as that of a border ranger, one of the King's men who police the kingdom near the Durncrag mountains of the west. He has been badly beaten and is nearly unconscious.

If you have the Kai Discipline of Hunting, turn to **297**.

If you do not, you must attack the Giaks now in order to save the ranger's life. Turn to **336**.

129

You reach the main gates of the capital, and stare in awe at the height of the city's walls. Two hundred feet high, the walls of Holmgard have withstood the ravages of both time and the Darklords. You and the officer race through the tunnel of the inner gatehouse, one hundred yards in length, and finally halt outside the doorway of the main watchtower. Great crowds of soldiers and civilians are running to and fro.

If you wish to continue following the officer, turn to **3**.

If you feel that you stand a better chance of making your way to the King's citadel on your own, turn to **144**.

130

You soon reach a small clearing in the woods. A bench, carved from a fallen tree is set in the centre of the clearing. You are hungry and must now eat a Meal here.

When you have finished, if you decide to leave the clearing by the south way, turn to **28**.

(contd over)

Or if you prefer the smaller track that leads east-wards into the forest, turn to **201**.

131 – *Illustration IX*

You have covered about a quarter of a mile when you hear shouting and a noise like thunderclaps ahead. Edging nearer, you soon make out a clearing that you recognize to be the site of the ruins of Raumas, an ancient forest temple.

A war party of Giaks, some twenty-five to thirty strong, are attacking the ruins from all sides. Many more of the Giaks are dead or dying among the broken pillars of marble, but still they assault whatever is hidden inside. Suddenly, a bolt of blue lightning rips through the front rank of Giaks sending the armour-clad creatures tumbling in all directions. A Giak, taller than the others and dressed from head to foot in black chainmail, curses at his troops as he whips them forward with a barbed flail.

With weapon ready, you move to the edge of the clearing, under cover of the thick foliage, and try to catch a glimpse of the defenders. To your amazement, the ruins are being defended by a young man no older than yourself. You recognize his sky-blue robes, embroidered with stars. He is a young

IX. A young theurgist of the Magicians Guild of Toran

theurgist of the Magicians Guild of Toran: an apprentice in magic.

Five Giaks charge forward, their spears raised to stab the apprentice as he hurriedly retreats deeper into the ruins. You see him turn and raise his left hand just before a bolt of blue flame shoots from his fingertips into the snarling Giak soldiers. Close to where you are hidden, you see a Giak scuttle past and climb one of the pillars of the temple. He has a long curved dagger in his mouth and he is about to jump on the young wizard standing below.

If you wish to shout a warning to the wizard, turn to **241**.

If you wish to run forward and attack the Giak when he jumps, turn to **55**.

If you wish to pick up a chunk of temple marble and throw it at the Giak's head, turn to **302**.

Or if you would rather turn and leave the battle area, and run back into the woods, turn to **101**.

132

The bodyguard looks at you with great suspicion and slams the door. You can hear voices chattering inside the caravan. Suddenly the door swings open and the face of a wealthy merchant appears. He recognizes your Kai cloak and apologizes for his servant's behaviour.

He says that they have been attacked several times since they left Toran: by Kraan, by bandits, and by robbers. They thought you may have been a bandit. Inside, the caravan is full of silks and spices. The merchant offers you food which you gratefully accept. After your sumptuous Meal, the fatigue of your ordeal finally overcomes you and you slip into a deep sleep.

Turn to **64**.

133

As you approach the statue, several cracks appear in its stone surface. It suddenly explodes before you as a real Winged Serpent breaks free of its stone mantle and attacks you.

You must fight the creature.

Winged Serpent: COMBAT SKILL 16   ENDURANCE 18

(This creature is immune to Mindblast.)

If you win the fight, turn to **266**.

134

Using your skills, you detect Giak tracks around the perimeter of the clearing. The prints are fresh and you can tell that these cruel minions of the Darklords were in this area less than two hours ago.

> Forewarned by this knowledge, if you decide to investigate the huts, turn to **305**.
> If you would rather avoid the clearing, turn to **40**.

135

Peering over the steep undercut of the river bank, you can see a tangle of driftwood along the water's edge. A large tree trunk has grounded on the clay bank next to a small canoe.

> If you wish to use the log to float down the river, turn to **223**.

(contd over)

If you wish to use the canoe, turn to **4**.

136

The Giaks get nearer and then crouch down as if preparing themselves to pounce. You can see the sharp serrated points of their spears and hear their low guttural speech. The larger of the two creatures screams, 'Orgadak taag! Nogjat aga ok!' and attacks you.

You must fight each of the Giaks in turn. Add 1 point to your COMBAT SKILL during this fight, as you have the advantage of the higher ground in your favour.

Giak 1: COMBAT SKILL 13   ENDURANCE 10
Giak 2: COMBAT SKILL 12   ENDURANCE 10

If you win, turn to **313**.

137

As the last of the foul creatures die, so the greenish light starts to fade. You notice that in each of the broken skulls lies a Gem. You take these 20 Gems before darkness engulfs the chamber. Remember to mark these on your *Action Chart*.

You quickly leave the dead Crypt spawn and press on.

Turn to **23**.

138

You prepare your weapon and advance to meet the enemy. There are two Mountain Giaks and you must fight them one at a time.

Giak 1: COMBAT SKILL 13   ENDURANCE 10
Giak 2: COMBAT SKILL 12   ENDURANCE 10

If you win, turn to **291**.

139

The inner courtyard is a bustle of activity. Cavalry scouts are waiting beside their nervous horses for messages from their unit commanders inside the Great Hall. They take orders with great speed to the defenders of the outer fieldworks. No sooner do they gallop off, than other scouts return, many of them breathless and wounded.

You have taken less than a dozen steps across the courtyard when you hear a deep voice boom out. 'Stop that man!'

Turn to **66**.

140

You are in a clearing where several trees have been cut down to make a rickety watchtower. Below the tower are three paths leading off in different directions.

If you take the south path, turn to **14**.
If you take the east path, turn to **252**.

(contd over)

If you take the southwest path, turn to **215**.
If you decide to climb the watchtower, turn to **36**.

141

Your Sixth Sense has warned you that some of the creatures that attacked the monastery are searching the two paths for any survivors of their raid, but you can avoid both tracks by making your way through the undergrowth of the woods.

If you wish to head south, turn to **56**.
Or if you wish to cut through the heavier foliage towards the northeast, turn to **333**.

142

You can see the tall grey-white walls and glimmering spires of Holmgard, its banners fluttering from the battlements in the fresh morning breeze. Stretching out towards the west, the River Eledil traces its course from the mountains of the Durncrag range to the Holmgulf. But from below the mountain peaks you can see a vast black army marching relentlessly on towards the city.

To your right you can see the highway heading off over the rolling plain towards Holmgard. At a run you could reach the outer fieldworks of the city defences in an hour, but you would be in the open for most of the time and vulnerable to attack by Kraan. However, ahead of you, a wide and muddy river drifts sluggishly towards the Eledil. You could use the cover of the river banks and swim towards the capital. Or towards your left lies the Graveyard of the Ancients. These tombs and crumbling monuments to a forgotten age would conceal your approach, but it is a forbidden area. Many are the unnamed horrors that lie there in restless sleep, waiting to consume the unwary trespasser.

If you will try your luck by the highway, turn to **58**.

If you feel that you stand a better chance of reaching the capital via the river, then turn to **135**.

Or if you are brave enough to risk the unknown perils of the Graveyard of the Ancients, turn to **102**.

143

You soon emerge from the woods onto a main highway. You recognize it as being the main road between the port of Toran in the north and the capital in the south. Spurring your horse on, you estimate you will reach the capital by morning.

Turn to **149**.

144

You fight your way through the press of bodies along the main street towards the citadel in the distance. City folk are rushing to and fro in the grip of panic, as the cries of Kraan are heard circling high above.

In the crush, one Item is stolen from your Backpack. If you no longer have a Backpack, you lose a Weapon. Remember to take this off your *Action Chart*.

A runaway horse and cart career past and knock you into a doorway. You are stunned and you lose 2 ENDURANCE points. As you stagger to your feet, the door bursts open and a decrepit old man attacks you with a meat cleaver. He is quite insane and you must fight him or take evasive action.

If you choose to fight, turn to **63**.
If you wish to evade a fight, turn to **217**.

145

You feel as if you have been run down by a cart or wagon. As you fall forward the last thing that you remember before the darkness overcomes you, is the taste of the sandy road and the terrible pain in your back.

Turn to **165**.

146

You have ridden about a mile when you are knocked from your horse by an arrow grazing your forehead. You lose 3 ENDURANCE points.

As you pull yourself to your feet, you see a patrol of Drakkarim emerge from the woods on either side of the road. You have been ambushed and must evade them as quickly as possible by going into the forest.

Turn to **154**.

147

After a few minutes walking, you find a mossy hut set

back from the path. You are hungry and must eat a Meal here or lose 3 ENDURANCE points. As you eat you notice that the path starts to curve towards the east.

If you wish to follow it, turn to **42**.
If you wish to return the way you have come, turn to **28**.

148

Kicking open the door, you dive into the farmhouse. A Kraan soars overhead, letting out a shriek of victory, a victim hanging in its claws. Getting to your feet, you find yourself alone. But propped against the fireplace is a Warhammer. You may take this Weapon if you wish.

If you want to stay in the farmhouse, turn to **81**.
If you would feel safer in the forest, you can make a dash by turning to **320**.
If you wish to search the room further, turn to **199**.

149

As you ride along the highway, you notice that light is getting worse. It will soon be completely dark – and impossible to see any dangers that may lurk ahead. You decide to hide and rest at the wood's edge until morning.

When you are satisfied that no one can see you, you pull your warm green cloak about you and drift off into an uneasy sleep.

Turn to **256**.

150

Although a little overcooked, the food tastes fine (although it is not enough for a whole Meal) and the clear water slakes your thirst. You have spent nearly half an hour resting in this house when you suddenly realize the delay.

Prepare your equipment and leave. Turn to **83**.

151

If you concentrate on the keyhole, you could move the mechanism of the lock and open it. You can then make the pin levitate and free it from the lockplate, avoiding falling prey to any traps that may be set off as the door unlocks.

If you wish to use your Kai Discipline of Mind Over Matter to open this lock and levitate the pin, turn to **87**.

152 – *Illustration X*

The herbalist offers you a selection of special potions. Some increase your strength; some induce invisibility; some give you great powers of stealth; and others give you the power of turning yourself into a gaseous form. The man pulls open the bottom drawer of the counter to reveal a magnificent wand. He says that it is a powerful weapon against all evil creatures, and that it will make you invulnerable in battle. He points to the mystical inscriptions which cover the black staff.

If you wish to lean over the counter and read the strange inscriptions, turn to **49**.

If you are more interested in the potions, turn to **231**.

X.   The herbalist offers you a selection of special potions

Before you are the tall grey-white walls and glimmering spires of Holmgard, the city's banners fluttering from the battlements in the fresh morning breeze. Stretching out towards the west, the River Eledil traces its course from the mountains of the Durncrag range to the Holmgulf. But below the mountain peaks you can see a vast black army marching relentlessly on towards the capital.

To your right you can see the highway heading off over the rolling plain towards Holmgard. At a gallop you could make the outer fieldworks of the city's defences in less than an hour, but you would be in the open for most of the time and vulnerable to attack by Kraan. Directly ahead of you, a wide river drifts sluggishly towards the Eledil. If you abandoned your horse, you could swim towards the outer defences under cover of the river banks. Or there is a final alternative. To your left lies the Graveyard of the Ancients. These tombs and crumbling monuments to a forgotten age would conceal your approach but it is a forbidden area. Many are the unnamed horrors that lie there in restless sleep, waiting to consume the unwary trespasser.

If you will try your luck by the highway, turn to **202**.

If you feel that you stand a better chance of reaching the capital via the river then turn to **135**.

Or if you are brave enough to risk the unknown perils of the Graveyard of the Ancients, turn to **329**.

154

You are dizzy from your wound and you stumble through the trees like a blind man.

Suddenly you fall forward as if the ground has been snatched from beneath your feet. You have fallen head first into a hunting pit. As you look up, you can see four Drakkarim levelling their bows at you, evil sneers spreading simultaneously across their ugly faces.

As the world darkens, the last thing you feel are the black shafts of their arrows deep in your chest. You have failed in your mission.

155

As you approach, the group of people stop talking. You can see by their expressions that they recognize your green Kai cloak. Slowly, one of the men extends his hand in friendship and says, 'My Lord, we had heard a rumour that the Kai were destroyed. Heaven be praised that it is not so. We feared all was lost.'

You do not tell them of the destruction of the monastery, for they are refugees from Toran and have lost everything they owned. Their only hope now is that the Kai Lords will lead an army to victory. You learn that the northern port was attacked from both air and sea, and that the forces of the Darklords far outnumbered the King's brave garrison. You reassure them that Sommerlund will not fall and wish them luck on their journey ahead.

Turn to **70**.

156

Black arrows embed themselves in the mud all around you. More Giaks have appeared on the steep slope of the river bank and are firing at you. There is no cover on this side of the river.

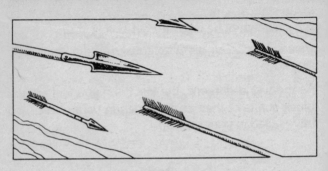

If you wish to dive into the water and swim with the current, turn to **294**.

If you wish to swim across to the cover of the trees on the other bank, turn to **245**.

157

The forest begins to thin out until finally you can make out a road through the trees ahead. The highway is full of people heading south. Many are wheeling their possessions along on handcarts.

If you wish to join the refugees and perhaps learn more of what has happened in the north, turn to **30**.

If you would prefer to continue to move south but under cover of the trees, turn to **167**.

158

The Key fits and the lock opens. You pull back the

door to find yourself face to face with a strange old man. In his right hand is a staff. Suddenly a bolt of lightning shoots from the staff and hits you square in the chest. You lose 6 ENDURANCE points. Gasping with pain, you knock the old man aside and run up the steep staircase towards daylight. You are halfway up the stairs when he fires another bolt at you.

Pick a number from the *Random Number Table*.

> If the number is *0–5*, the bolt misses you and shatters part of the wall.
>
> If the number is *6–9*, then you have been hit in the back and lose a further 4 ENDURANCE points.
>
> If you survive, you stagger out into the daylight and curse your bad luck. It was only by an unlucky chance you discovered the secret temple of a sect of evil druids. You are very lucky to have escaped with your life. You quickly rejoin the path which now disappears over the hill.

Turn to **106**.

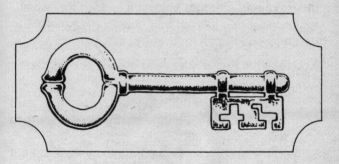

159

Your ploy does not work, for the merchant will not allow you to enter his caravan. Suddenly he clicks his fingers and the bodyguard grasps the hilt of his scimitar.

You must fight him by turning to **191**.

Or you must jump clear of the speeding caravan. Turn to **234**.

160

Pick a number from the *Random Number Table*.

If it is *0–4*, you have been seen. Turn to **286**.

If it is *5–9*, they do not spot you and they slowly file away along the far side of the ridge. Turn to **10**.

161

As you sit down, the stone serpent slowly moves forward on its plinth. You suddenly break out in a cold sweat and grasp your weapon with trembling fingers in case it should attack. A red forked tongue appears from the head of this strange statue and dips into the bowl of green light above your head. Slowly the tongue re-emerges holding a Golden Key which, to your surprise, it drops into your lap. A panel in the east wall clicks open to reveal an exit.

You take the Key and leave as quickly as possible.

Turn to **209**.

162

As you get nearer to the men, you call to them. As they turn to face you, your skin turns cold and your heart pounds, for they are Drakkarim in disguise. Suddenly they charge at you. Forced to the ground, you are tied up with ropes and dragged behind them along a track. They take your Backpack and Weapons, but do not search your cloak or find your Gold Crowns. They cackle menacingly to themselves, and talk at great length of the tortures that await you at their camp.

If you have the Kai Discipline of Mind Over Matter, turn to **258**.

If you do not have this skill, turn to **127**.

163

After nearly an half an hour you feel the current getting stronger. Looking out across the surface you can see that you are approaching a whirlpool in the middle of a large river bend. You will surely drown if caught in its current, so you quickly swim towards the right hand river bank and continue your mission on foot, carrying all your equipment.

Turn to **321**.

164

Carefully opening the seals on each of the bottles, you sniff at the contents. They all seem to be different types of wine. Suddenly a smaller bottle tucked behind the others catches your eye. Pulling out the glass stopper, you recognize the smell to be that of Alether, a Potion of Strength, which is orange in colour.

You may keep this Potion and swallow it before you fight. It will increase your COMBAT SKILL by 2 points for the duration of your fight. Be sure to mark it down on your *Action Chart* and to strike it off once you have used it.

You now decide to investigate the stable by turning to **308**.

165

You awake in a fever. Images swim before your eyes and then fade completely. The pain in your back is intense and you cry out for relief. You feel a cool, damp cloth placed on your forehead and glimpse the worried face of a young woman. An old man whispers in her ear and then he disappears from view. The girl kneels at your side and comforts you with words of kindness and reassurance, but the light quickly fades and darkness engulfs you once more.

Turn to **212**.

166

You are in the presence of a great evil. Your mind is being probed by a powerful and timeless being and you must shield yourself. The struggle has begun and your sanity is at stake. It is a long and tortuous ordeal, during which you experience many fantastic and terrible apparitions that tempt and appal you. After this you must lose 4 ENDURANCE points and stagger towards the tunnel.

Turn to **104**.

167

You have been travelling for about a mile when you notice two legs sticking out from behind a large boulder.

If you wish to take a closer look, turn to **88**.

If you would rather avoid meeting their owner and press on into the forest, turn to **264**.

If you possess and wish to use the Kai Discipline of Sixth Sense, turn to **178**.

168

You pull yourself to the top of the opulent caravan and nestle among the travelling cases and bags. Night will soon engulf the highway. A chill wind blows from the west and you pull your cloak around yourself to keep warm. You listen to the voices below and you can smell the mouthwatering aroma of spiced meat. It reminds you that you are very hungry and must now take a Meal.

The fatigue of your ordeal finally catches up with you and you drift off into a restless sleep.

Turn to **64**.

169

As you pass each skull, it slowly turns, as if watching your every move. You are halfway across the room when you hear the sharp crack of bone splitting. Suddenly you see hideous shapes hatching inside the skulls, and stretching their wings.

Ten slimy winged creatures attack you, and you must fight them as one enemy.

Crypt Spawn: COMBAT SKILL 16   ENDURANCE 16

You may evade more fighting after the first round of combat and run for the archway by turning to **23**.

If you win the combat, turn to **137**.

170 – *Illustration XI*

The tunnel is dark and the air is much cooler than outside. You carefully advance with one hand on the tunnel wall to aid your sense of direction. You have been in total darkness for three minutes when you detect the foul smell of decay ahead, similar to rotting meat. If you have a Torch and Tinderbox in your Pack, you may light the Torch to see your way ahead.

Suddenly, something heavy drops from the tunnel ceiling onto your back and you fall to your knees. It is a Burrowcrawler and you must fight it, for it is trying to strangle you with its long slimy tentacles.

Burrowcrawler: COMBAT SKILL 17   ENDURANCE 7

If you do not have a torch, deduct 3 points from your COMBAT SKILL during this fight. The Burrowcrawler is immune to Mindblast and Animal Kinship.

If you win, turn to **319**.

171

You are at the very edge of the wood when your horse rears up in agony. The Kraan has sunk its claws deep into the horse's hind legs and is trying to knock you to the ground with its wings. The ghoulish Giak rider squeals with delight as he stabs at you with his spear. You jump to the ground and dash for the trees, leaving the poor dying horse in the clutches of the Kraan.

Turn to **303**.

XI.   It is a Burrowcrawler and it is trying to strangle you

172

Night falls and you are soon engulfed in darkness. To press on any further would be futile, for you would be sure to lose your way. Tethering your horse to a tree, you pull your green Kai cloak about you and fall into a restless sleep.

You are awoken by the sound of troops in the distance. Across the lake you see the black shapes of Drakkarim and a pack of Doomwolves. A Kraan appears from above the trees and lands on the roof of the small wooden shack. It is being ridden by a creature dressed in red robes. The Kraan takes off and begins to fly across the lake to where you are hidden.

If you wish to ride deeper into the forest to escape the Kraan, turn to **239**.

If you wish to use the Kai Discipline of Camouflage to hide yourself and your horse, turn to **114**.

If you wish to prepare to fight the creature, turn to **29**.

173

As you reach the door you hear the crash of a giant stone slab as it falls from the ceiling. Turning around, you see that your exit is now blocked.

If you have a Silver Key, you may try to open the door by turning to **158**.

If you do not possess a Silver Key, turn to **259**.

174

After nearly an hour of drifting downstream, the water current becomes quite strong and you can see that you are being drawn towards a whirlpool near the centre as the river curves round. You know that if you are caught in the swirling water, you stand very little chance of escaping a watery death. You dive into the muddy river and as you begin to swim towards the shore you unfortunately lose your Backpack and Weapons. Without your equipment, you reach the wooded bank.

Turn to **190**.

175

Waving your arms at the approaching cavalry, you recognize them to be border rangers of the King's army, tough woodsmen who police the troubled western frontier of the kingdom. Your relief at seeing them soon fades when you realize that they are fleeing from a pack of Doomwolves with snarling Giak riders. Black arrows are dropping all around the rangers, as the vicious Doomwolves get nearer and nearer.

If you wish to take cover and hide, turn to **41**.

If you wish to make for the other bank, turn to **116**.

If you possess the Kai Discipline of Camouflage, turn to **182**.

176

You hide behind some thick bushes so that the Doomwolf and its rider will not see your white horse. Luckily it works – the beast lopes past and vanishes down the track that you have just come along.

If you wish to attack the remaining Doomwolves and their riders, turn to **253**.

(contd over)

If you wish to press on deeper into the forest, turn to **126**.

177

You search all of the cupboards in the small cottage but do not find anything of use or value. You decide that you have wasted enough time here and must press on without further delay.

Turn to **83**.

178

Your skill enables you to recognize the boots and leggings of a King's soldier. You can sense that the man is wounded and in need of help.

If you wish to aid him, turn to **88**.
If you would rather leave him here, turn to **264**.

179

You have been spotted by the guards who level their crossbows at you.

If you wish to raise your hands above your head and walk slowly towards them, turn to **318**.

If you wish to run for cover in the trees, turn to **51**.

180

They see you raise your weapon, and they instantly attack you.

If you decide to fight them, you must fight them one at a time.

> Leader: COMBAT SKILL 15   ENDURANCE 22
> Soldier 1: COMBAT SKILL 13   ENDURANCE 20
> Soldier 2: COMBAT SKILL 12   ENDURANCE 20

If you kill all three of them, turn to **62**.
If you wish to evade combat, turn to **22**.

181

Instinctively you duck, and dive to avoid the cross-bow bolt. The bandit fires and you feel the sleeve of your jacket tear as the missile grazes past your left arm. You thank the gods for your good fortune and sprint on.

None of the other bandits have bows and they soon give up the chase. As you sprint off into the distance, you leave them all far behind. You have lost your Weapons and Equipment, but not your life.

You stop just long enough to strap up your wounded arm and then continue along the road towards the outer defences of the capital.

Turn to **288**.

182

Three rangers gallop past the river bank, closely followed by the Giaks on their snarling mounts – the

Doomwolves. But your Camouflage skill has saved you from being spotted. The pack of evil Giaks continue on their chase without even glancing at the river.

Turn to **174**.

183

The officer orders his men to halt and asks you your business. You tell him who you are, and how the monastery has been destroyed. He is deeply saddened to hear your news. He offers you a horse and asks you to accompany him to Prince Pelathar, the King's son.

If you accept, turn to **97**.
If you decide to decline his offer, turn to **200**.

184

The caravan is out of control and is bumping wildly through the rough ground that borders the highway. With difficulty you eventually steer the frightened horses back onto the road and halt the caravan.

A quick search of the interior reveals 40 Gold Crowns, a Sword and enough Food for 4 Meals. If you wish to keep any of these items, mark them on your *Action Chart*.

The fatigue of your ordeal finally catches up with you. You must eat a Meal after which you fall into a deep sleep.

Turn to **64**.

185

You narrow your eyes and scan the trees for some

sign of the hidden archer. Your wait is not a long one, for a moment later a sharp pain tears through your chest and you are thrown back by the force of three arrows. Two of the black shafts have sunk deep into your rib cage, and the third has pierced your thigh.

The last thing that you see is the canopy of fern trees above and a large green dragonfly as it settles on your belt buckle.

Your life and your mission end here.

186

The Kakarmi disappear into the dense undergrowth and you soon find yourself lost. After nearly two hours of walking you hear the sound of running water. You decide to investigate a little closer.

Turn to **106**.

187

Two furry faces appear over the top of the trunk. Both pairs of eyes stare at your weapon and the two creatures let out a shriek of fright. Leaping from the trunk, they disappear into the forest.

If you wish to follow them, turn to **186**.

If you wish to let them go and continue, turn to **228**.

188

You can see the shadow of the Kraan getting larger all around you. It suddenly strikes, pitching you forward onto your face with the power of its attack.

Pick a number from the *Random Number Table*.

If the number you have picked is 0–6, the Kraan has ripped away your Backpack. You have lost the Pack and all the Equipment that was inside it.

If the number picked is 7–9, your Backpack is intact but you have been wounded in both arms. Lose 3 ENDURANCE points and run to the trees.

Now turn to **303**.

189

You thank your Kai training and your quick thinking, for that bog could have proved as deadly as any Drakkarim or Kraan.

You are worried about losing time, and push on further into the trees towards the south. Ahead of you, you see a wide path that also leads south.

Turn to **118**.

190

You walk for three miles along the water's edge until you chance upon a wrecked river barge. It appears to have served as shelter for someone, as you can see a bed and some cooking utensils through a hole in the deck.

If you wish to search the barge, turn to **20**.
If you wish to press on, turn to **273**.

191

The bodyguard unsheathes a large scimitar and strikes at your head.

Bodyguard: COMBAT SKILL 11   ENDURANCE 21

If you win, turn to **24**.
If you wish to evade more combat during the fight, you can jump from the speeding caravan by turning to **234**.

192

You see the razor-fanged mouth of a Doomwolf and hear the hideous cries of the Giaks. Two of them are coming straight for you. You are saved from certain death when your horse jumps at the approaching beasts, knocking them both to the ground. You lash out at the Giak and open a large wound in his head . . . and then suddenly, as if by a miracle, you're through and racing on down the highway, clear of the rest of the pack.

But a shadow follows you. It is a Kraan and it has started to dive. Its target is you.

> If you veer off the highway towards the cover of the trees, turn to **171**.
>
> If you press on regardless of the Kraan, and gallop flat out down the highway, turn to **120**.

193

The beast and its rider lie dead. You notice a Scroll tucked into the Giak's belt. You may take this if you wish, but remember to mark it on your *Action Chart*. The other Doomwolves are charging along the path towards you.

> If you wish to fight them, turn to **253**.
>
> If you wish to escape into the woods, turn to **126**.

194

You sprint towards the wagon. People are running everywhere in panic as the Kraan make their attack, carrying their poor victims off into the darkening sky. A large Kraan is hovering above the wagon and three snarling Giaks drop from its back onto the startled horses. You must fight them or leave the wagon and run to the safety of a nearby farmhouse.

> If you wish to fight the Giaks, turn to **208**.
>
> If you wish to run to the farmhouse, turn to **148**.

195

Wiping the bear's blood from your weapon, you notice the mouth of a cave hidden behind the rock from which the bear attacked.

If you wish to investigate this cave further, turn to **59**.
If you wish to press on, turn to **106**.

196

You follow the man into a small library off the main hall. He pushes one of the many books on the shelves which line all four walls, and you hear a metallic click. One section of the bookcase slowly slides back to reveal a hidden passage.

If you wish to follow the man into the passage, turn to **332**.

If you do not want to enter the dark corridor, leave the guildhall and return to the street. Turn to **144**.

197

The Drakkar lies dead at the bottom of the ferry. He has a Short Sword and 6 Gold Crowns which you may keep if you wish . You push the body into the water where it floats for a few seconds before disappearing into the icy depths.

Grabbing the pole, you steer to the other side of the lake and abandon the ferry.

Turn to **172**.

198

You can sense that there is someone else behind the screen. There is a lingering aura of wickedness around this shop. Be on your guard – something is wrong here.

If you wish to return to the street, turn to **7**.

If you wish to examine the goods in the glass counter, turn to **152**.

199

Most of the cupboards and drawers are empty. Whoever lived here took nearly everything they owned with them, but you do manage to scrape together enough fruit in the cellar for one Meal. You may mark this on your *Action Chart*.

Turn to **81**.

200 – *Illustration XII*

Night is starting to close in. The shadows of the forest are growing longer and darker. Just as you are about to stop and rest, you see through the trees a line of people moving south along a wide highway. Moving closer, you notice a large merchant's caravan in the centre of the dusty turnpike. It is drawn by six large horses and is moving much faster than any of the other traffic. This could be your chance to reach the capital as quickly as possible.

If you wish to jump onto the caravan, turn to **78**.

If you wish to use the Kai Discipline of Camouflage to hide in among the packing cases strapped to the roof, turn to **168**.

201

You follow the rough track for nearly an hour when you notice ahead of you another wider path branching off towards the south.

If you wish to turn south along the new path, turn to **238**.

But if you wish to head east, turn to **215**.

Or if you wish to go west, turn to **130**.

XII.   You notice a large merchant's caravan in the centre of the
dusty turnpike

202

Urging your horse forward, you gallop down the long stretch of highway towards the capital. After only a few minutes your horse suddenly slows and finally limps to a halt. You dismount and examine its raised right foreleg. You curse your ill luck, for you see that it has thrown a shoe and injured its hoof quite badly. You will have to leave him here and proceed on foot as quickly as you can.

Turn to **58**.

203

You suddenly feel a searing pain shoot through your chest as something explodes against you in a shower of red sparks.

You lose 10 ENDURANCE points. Through the smoke, the Sage is preparing to throw more explosive at you.

If you have 10 or more ENDURANCE points left, turn to **80**.

If you now have less than 10 ENDURANCE points, turn to **344**.

204

After an hour of walking you arrive at a junction. The path continues south and another path joins it from the west. You realize that the west path will lead you back to the marsh, so you continue southwards.

Turn to **111**.

205

Their leader picks up your discarded Equipment and ushers you along the road ahead. An evil grin spreads across the face of the other two men, and you suddenly realize that they are not soldiers after all. You make a break for it and run away from them, sprinting towards the distant capital.

Behind you, the ominous click of a crossbow being primed sends a shiver down your spine.

Pick a number from the *Random Number Table*.

If the number you have picked is *0–4*, turn to **181**.
If the number is *5–9*, turn to **145**.

206

The path soon joins a highway where a signpost indicates Toran to the north and Holmgard to the south. You turn south towards the capital.

Turn to **224**.

207

The track soon reaches a larger road which crosses the stream via a stone bridge. A signpost at the bridge points north to Toran and south to Holmgard. The road itself is jammed with people moving south, some pushing their possessions along on handcarts. You join the refugee column and head towards the capital.

Turn to **30**.

208

The ghoulish creatures thrust their spears at you and attack. Fight these creatures as a single enemy.

Giaks: COMBAT SKILL 15   ENDURANCE 13

If you win, you can run to the safety of the farmhouse by turning to **148**.

Or you can return to the woods. Turn to **320**.

209

You see ahead a corridor sloping upwards, and as you reach the top of this slope, a stone portal slides across to reveal another passage ahead.

You step through the opening which then quickly closes with a crunch.

Turn to **23**.

210

Just inside the door, you are stopped by a journeyman of the Guildhall and asked to explain your intrusion. You calmly inform him of your urgent message for the King, and he hurries you into the Guildmaster's chambers.

A distinguished old man in deep purple robes turns to greet you and listens to your story. Taking you by the arm, he leads you into an adjoining library and closes the door. Pressing one of the many thousands of books, he releases a secret panel in the wall and beckons you to follow him.

If you wish to follow him into the dark passage, turn to **332**.

If you are not completely happy about this man and wish to leave the Guildhall, turn to **37**.

211

You walk along a dimly lit corridor which opens out into a large square room, with an oak door in the far wall.

If you wish to walk across to the door, turn to **173**.

If you possess the Kai Discipline of Sixth Sense turn to **244**.

If you would prefer to return to the surface and continue your journey, turn to **106**.

212 – *Illustration XIII (overleaf)*

When you awake, the pain is but a memory. Restore all lost ENDURANCE points to your original score. A tall man dressed in white robes stands before you, a bowl of herbs in his hands. Placing the leaves into a kettle of boiling water, he then turns to greet you.

'You have passed close to death and have seen his face, Kai Lord, but the Grey One has not claimed you for his flock. You are healed in body but I sense that you are wounded in spirit. What is it that troubles you so?'

You recognize the man to be one of the King's senior

physicians, for the gold embroidered emblem of a dove upon his sleeve is the sign of his respected vocation. You tell the aged cleric of the events at the monastery and of your perilous journey to the King.

Raising you gently from the bed by your arm, he bids you follow him. You notice that you are in a lavishly decorated room which leads out through a long corridor lined with tapestries. It slowly dawns on you just where you are.

This is the citadel of Holmgard and you are about to meet the King.

Turn to **350**.

213

You have been trudging through the forest for nearly two hours. The nagging fear that you are lost begins to seem a reality. Apart from the occasional cry of a Kraan in the far distance, you have seen or heard no evidence that the enemy is in this part of the forest. As you descend a rocky hillock, you see something unusual in the tangled woods ahead.

Turn to **331**.

214

The path gradually narrows until it disappears completely into a mass of dense vegetation. You cannot go any further on this route and therefore you must return to the clearing.

Turn to **125** and take the south path.

215

You emerge into a small clearing. In the centre you

XIII.   A tall man dressed in white robes stands before you, a
bowl of herbs in his hands

see the skeletal remains of a large animal. To the south a narrow track leads off into the distance.

If you wish to examine the skeleton, turn to **346**.
If you would rather press on, turn to **14**.

216

Placing one hand on his forehead and the other on his wounded arm, you feel the warmth of your healing powers leave your body and give strength to the injured man.

He tells you his name is Trimis and he is a soldier in Prince Pelathar's army. The Prince and his troops are engaged in battle to the south, where a large force of the Darklords' creatures are attacking the bridge of Alema. During the fight, he had been snatched into the air by a Kraan, and dropped into the forest.

You make the soldier as comfortable as possible before continuing on your mission.

Turn to **264**.

217

You quickly escape from the madman and dodge along a dark alleyway where the houses are small and cramped together. At the very end is a green door with a sign above it that says:

If you wish to enter, turn to **91**.

If you wish to wait until you are sure the madman has disappeared and then return to the main street, turn to **7**.

218

Your senses reveal that more than just horses are heading towards you. You can just make out the very high shrieks of Giak war cries in the distance. By the number of cries and curses you estimate that there are over a dozen Giaks, and probably Doomwolves as well. You decide that advertising your existence is perhaps not quite such a good idea after all!

Turn to **75**.

219

All that remains of you now is embedded five feet into the stairs on which you were standing, beneath a vast granite block.

Your mission and your life end here.

220

The bodyguard unsheathes a scimitar and lunges for your head.

Bodyguard: COMBAT SKILL 11   ENDURANCE 20

If you win, turn to **24**.
If you wish to evade combat at any time during the fight, you can jump from the speeding caravan by turning to **234**.

221

Cautiously, you approach the base of the log wall. The tree trunks are rough hewn and afford plenty of footholds for your climb. As you reach the top of the wall, you come face to face with a crossbow. The soldier holding it in your face motions for you to descend a wooden ladder to the ground. You do not argue with him. Slowly you descend the ladder.

Turn to **318**.

222

As you go on you discover a forest path that divides at the point you join it.

If you wish to take the south fork, turn to **140**.
If you wish to take the east fork, turn to **252**.
If you wish to use your Kai Discipline of Tracking, turn to **67**.

223

After quite a struggle, you manage to free the heavy trunk from the river bank. Gathering your equipment in a bundle, you stow it on top of the log and then slowly wade out into the river. The current soon takes you and you drift slowly downstream.

After twenty minutes you hear the sound of horses along the left bank.

If you wish to hide behind the log, turn to **75**.
If you wish to climb onto the log and prepare to catch the riders' attention, then turn to **175**.

224

You have ridden several miles and have seen no sign of refugees or of the enemy. You race on towards a high ridge in the middle distance. You should be able to see the capital from there.

As you reach the peak, the sight that meets you on the far side is one of hope – but there is still one challenge you know you have to face.

Turn to **153**.

225

You recognize the language to be that of the Kakarmi, an intelligent race of forest animals that live in, and care for the forests of Sommerlund. You have nothing to fear from these creatures as they are very timid and gentle in their behaviour. Using your skill of Animal Kinship, you call to them in their strange native tongue.

If you say 'Do not be afraid, I am a friend,' turn to **187**.

If you say 'I am a Kai Lord. I wish you no harm. I must talk with you,' turn to **39**.

226

At first the descent is quite easy, but you soon find it dificult to see clearly and your legs feel very weak. The 'Sleeptooth' scratches are affecting you, and suddenly you pitch forward and slip head first into darkness.

Pick a number from the *Random Number Table*.

If the number you have picked is 0–4, turn to **277**.
If the number is 5–9, turn to **338**.

227

You are now up to your waist in slimy water. The air is thick with small insects that sting your face and clog your nose. Something wraps itself around your leg. It is a Marshviper and you must fight it.

Marshviper: COMBAT SKILL 16   ENDURANCE 6

If you lose any ENDURANCE points in the combat, turn to **271**.

If you kill it without losing any ENDURANCE points, turn to **348**.

228

The path continues eastwards but soon disappears into thick undergrowth.

If you continue east, cutting through the vegetation with your axe, turn to **140**.

If you head south to where the bushes are less dense, and then press on through the forest, turn to **215**.

229

The Kraan hovers above you, raising dust with the beat of its huge black wings. The dust gets into your eyes and nose, and you start to cough. Now the beast attacks.

You must fight it to the death. Because of the dust, you must reduce your COMBAT SKILL by 1 point.

Kraan: COMBAT SKILL 16   ENDURANCE 25

If you win you have a choice.
Will you search the body by turning to **267**?
Or will you continue along the east path by turning to **125**?

230

In the far distance, you can make out the silhouette of soldiers on barges that are strung out in a line across the river. You can hear the low growls of Doom-wolves returning along the opposite bank.

For once you throw caution to the wind and sprint along the river bank towards the barges in the distance.

Turn to **179**.

231

You are about to ask the price of the potions when the bamboo screen crashes down and a young man leaps at you. He has a long curved dagger in his hand.

He is upon you and you must fight for your life.

Robber: COMBAT SKILL 13   ENDURANCE 20

If you kill him within 4 rounds of combat, turn to **94**.
If you are still fighting after 4 rounds of combat, turn to **203**.
You may evade more fighting after 2 rounds of combat by dashing through the front door. If you wish to do this, turn to **7**.

232

The rough-looking leader approaches you and says, 'Our needs are simple, kind sir. Your money or your life!'

If you wish to fight them, turn to **180**.
If you wish to run, turn to **22**.

233

After nearly an hour, you catch up with the horse and succeed in calming him down. You are now north of the cabin, but you are confident of finding your way back.

Mounting the horse, you ride back past the cabin, and press on towards the south once again.

Turn to **206**.

234

You jump clear of the speeding caravan but land very badly and break your ankle. The pain is terrible and you soon lose consciousness.

Unfortunately you never wake up, but it may be of interest to you that your head is now adorning the saddle of a Kraan.

Your life and your mission end here.

235

The Prince's horse is indeed a magnificent animal, fast and sure of foot. You gallop along the twisting track as if it were a straight highway, until the noise of battle has disappeared far behind you.

You are hungry and must eat a Meal during your ride.

After several miles, the path stops abruptly at a junction. There is a signpost, but it has been hacked down.

If you wish to turn left, go to **32**.
If you wish to turn right, go to **146**.
If you wish to use your Kai Discipline of Tracking, turn to **254**.

236

The Gem hovers above the mouth of the skeleton king, glowing a fierce red. Suddenly, an explosion of searing crimson flame lashes upwards from the sarcophagus, destroying the Gem completely. You are thrown against the far wall and knocked unconscious.

When you awake, the chamber is completely empty. The skeleton king and the sarcophagus have vanished. You have lost 6 ENDURANCE points, and your initial COMBAT SKILL is reduced by 1 point for the rest of your life.

You carefully get to your feet and stagger towards the tunnel.

Turn to **104**.

237

You make full use of your Kai Discipline and quickly burrow deep into the loose earth of the wooded hillside. Covering yourself with your cloak, you pull a loose branch across your hastily dug shelter.

Pick a number from the *Random Number Table*.

If you have picked a number *0–4*, then you have passed undetected. Turn to **265**.

If you have picked a number *5–9*, then you are not so lucky! Turn to **72**.

238

The path meanders between several small, wooded hills and eventually leads to a ruined log cabin. It seems that it had burnt down not so long ago, for the ashes are still warm and a haze of smoke still lingers. You sense possible danger here.

You may leave by the south route by turning to **42**. Or you may take the north track by turning to **68**.

239

As you push on into the forest, you hear the wings of the Kraan pass above the trees and disappear northwards. You ride on for nearly an hour until you come to a clearing. On the far side is a track that leads off to the south.

> If you wish to enter the clearing and take the south exit, turn to **34**.
>
> If you would rather skirt the edge of the clearing and pick up the track further on, turn to **118**.

240

The path leads along a ridge of wooded hillocks and changes direction towards the east.

> Turn to **79**.

241

The wizard heeds your cry and spins around just in time to loose a searing bolt of energy at the Giak. The creature's head disintegrates in flames and its twitching body falls in a heap at the foot of the pillar. The Giak officer sees you and shouts, 'Ogot . . . Ogot!' to his cowering troops, who quickly run away from the ruins to the safety of the forest beyond.

The young wizard wipes his brow, and walks towards you, his hand extended in gratitude and friendship.

> Turn to **349**.

242

The lid of the sarcophagus slips to the floor with a dull crunch. You are looking at the remains of an ancient king, who lies still surrounded by his treasure. An ornate crown is still in position on his skull. The jaw of the skeleton is wide open and the darkness of the mouth seems strangely bottomless. A distant rumbling can now be heard from deep in the earth.

If you have the Kai Discipline of Mindshield, turn to **166**.

If you do not, turn to **9**.

243

Hurrying through the forest, you stumble and fall down a steep slope which drops you in a heap on a hidden path below. On the path is a dead body. It is a Giak, a spiteful and ghoulish servant of the Darklords. Many centuries ago, their ancestors were used by the Darklords to build for them the infernal city of Helgedad, which lies in the volcanic wastelands beyond the Durncrag range of mountains. The construction of the city was a long and torturous nightmare, and only the strongest of the Giaks survived the heat and poisonous atmospheres of Helgedad. This creature that lies before you is a descendant of these Giak slaves. It has been killed by a sword blow to its head, and by its side lies a Mace. You may take this Weapon if you wish.

Continue along the hidden path by turning to **97**.

244

Your senses tell you that you are not alone. You are in very great danger. Return to the surface as quickly as you can.

Turn to **93**.

245

Arrows hit the water above you, and drop harmlessly past as you swim beneath the surface towards the opposite bank.

XIV. He laughs menacingly and pulls back the hood of his cloak. He is a Drakkar and you must fight him

Quickly you wade out of the river and dash for the trees. You are now out of range of the Giaks, who remount their Doomwolves and continue their chase.

Turn to **190**.

246 – *Illustration XIV (previous page)*

When the ferry reaches the middle of the lake, the man stops rowing and stands up. He laughs menacingly and pulls back the hood of his cloak to reveal himself. He is a Drakkar and you must fight him.

Drakkar: COMBAT SKILL 15   ENDURANCE 23

If you win, turn to **197**.

247

The merchant looks angry. He calls to his bodyguard. You must think of something quickly.

If you decide to offer him something of greater value that you have in your Backpack, turn to **159**.

If you prepare to fight the bodyguard, turn to **220**.

248

You reach the base of the hill and hurry into the forest. After only a few minutes you discover an old forest track.

If you wish to follow this track north, turn to **44**.

If you wish to follow this track east, turn to **300**.

249

You descend a flight of stone stairs that lead to a large chamber. A macabre sight awaits you. Directly opposite, across the large stone room, is an ornate archway with a corridor leading into the darkness beyond. The strange green light radiates from two lines of skulls each resting on a stone plinth. They face each other to form an eerie walkway across the room.

If you wish to walk across the room to the archway, turn to **169**.

If you wish to attack the skulls, turn to **107**.

250

Leaping from the top of the trunk, you land in front of two small furry creatures. You recognize that they are Kakarmi, an intelligent race of animals that inhabit, and tend the forests of Sommerlund. Before you can apologize for your dramatic entrance, the frightened little creatures scurry off into the forest.

If you wish to follow them, turn to **186**.

If you wish to continue, turn to **228**.

251

You are lucky, they do not seem to have spotted you. They slowly move on and have soon disappeared along the far side of the ridge. You continue your run.

Turn to **10**.

252

In the centre of a small clearing you see a group of humans talking excitedly and gesturing wildly with their hands. There are two children, three men and a woman. Their belongings are wrapped in bundles which they carry slung over their shoulders. Their clothes look well made and expensive but they are dirty and torn.

If you wish to approach them and ask who they are, turn to **155**.

If you wish to avoid them and continue onwards on your mission, turn to **70**.

253

The Doomwolves are soon on you and you must fight them one at a time.

Doomwolf 1: COMBAT SKILL 13   ENDURANCE 24
Doomwolf 2: COMBAT SKILL 14   ENDURANCE 23
Doomwolf 3: COMBAT SKILL 14   ENDURANCE 22
Doomwolf 4: COMBAT SKILL 15   ENDURANCE 21

If you kill them all in battle, turn to **278**.

254

Your Tracking ability tells you that several trails from the right path lead off in the direction of the left path. They have been made by large wolves. The Dark-lords use such beasts to scout for their armies. They are vicious creatures and are often ridden by Giaks. The left path leads towards Holmgard, and the right path leads off towards the Durncrag mountains. The choice of route is yours.

If you wish to turn left, go to **32**.
If you wish to turn right, go to **146**.

255

The creature that you now face is a Gourgaz, one of a race of cold-blooded reptilian creatures that dwell deep in the treacherous Maakenmire swamps. Their favourite food is human flesh!

The Prince's Sword lies at your feet. You may pick up and use this weapon if you wish. The Gourgaz is about to strike at you – you must fight him to the death.

Gourgaz: COMBAT SKILL 20   ENDURANCE 30

This creature is immune to Mindblast.

If you win, turn to **82**.

256

You are awoken by the cries of Kraan high above you in the clear morning sky. Rubbing your eyes, you peer upwards through the canopy of branches to see three of the loathsome creatures fly off towards the north.
You are sure you have not been spotted, but perhaps it would be best to leave now – just in case. You mount your horse and ride south along the highway.

Turn to **224**.

257

You find a stone portal in the east wall, but there does not appear to be any way of opening it.

If you wish to examine the statue, turn to **133**.
If you wish to sit on the seat, turn to **161**.

258

Using your Kai Discipline of Mind Over Matter, you untie the ropes binding your hands. You wait for a chance to make a break for it and then sprint as fast as you can into the dense undergrowth. Black arrows whistle past you, but you are soon deep among the trees and safe again. You have lost your Backpack and Weapons but you have your life and limbs intact. You continue to push on into the forest.

Turn to **50**.

259

The room is getting colder. You gradually notice the smell of sulphur in the air. You can hear chanting in the distance. It sounds as if it is somewhere in another part of this cave. A slit in the stone wall opens, and the end of a black staff begins to appear. Suddenly a bolt of blue lightning leaps from the staff and hits you in the chest.

As your life slowly drains away, the last thing you see is an old man dressed in black robes raising a dagger above your throat.

Your life and your mission end here.

260

Swimming towards the bank, you can see the ranger spreadeagled at the water's edge. You reach him but only to find that he has broken his neck in the fall and is dead.

Suddenly, two Giaks jump on you from above and you must fight them. You are unarmed and must fight the Giaks with your bare hands. Deduct 4 points from your COMBAT SKILL and fight them one at a time.

Giak 1: COMBAT SKILL 11   ENDURANCE 18
Giak 2: COMBAT SKILL 12   ENDURANCE 17

If you win, turn to **156**.

261

Sweating, and out of breath, you part the dense undergrowth to see a Kraan hovering over the wagon. Three ghoulish Giaks drop from its back, startling the horses. They advance upon the helpless children with their spears.

If you wish to run back to the wagon and defend the children, turn to **208**.

If you want to run deeper into the forest, turn to **264**.

262

The merchant takes your Gold and clicks his fingers. His bodyguard attacks you with his scimitar.

If you wish to fight, turn to **191**.

If you wish to evade combat, jump clear of the speeding caravan by turning to **234**.

263

Carefully, you follow the stream as it makes its way towards the east. Suddenly you notice something in the distance that brings you to a halt.

Lying in the rushing water like a great black dam is a dead Kraan. You creep nearer, under cover of the foliage, until you see three arrows deep in the beast's chest. Trapped beneath the beast is the body of its rider. It is a Giak, a spiteful and malicious servant of the Darklords. Many centuries ago, their ancestors were used by the Darklords to build the infernal city of Helgedad, which lies in the volcanic wastelands beyond the Durncrag range of mountains. The construction of the city was a long and torturous nightmare, and only the strongest Giaks survived the heat and poisonous atmospheres of Helgedad. This creature is a descendant of these Giak slaves. It seems that this one must have drowned. The Giak's pouch contains 3 Gold Crowns. (You may take these if you wish.)

You may continue downstream, by turning to **70**.
Or you may leave the stream and make your way on foot through the wooded hills to the south by turning to **157**.

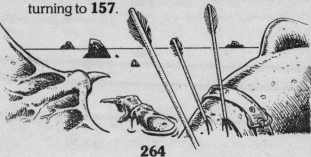

264

You have not gone far when you hear the sound of battle to the west.

If you wish to follow the sound, turn to **97**.
If you would rather continue south, turn to **6**.

265

You quickly move off into the forest before more Doomwolves or Kraan appear.

You have walked for more than an hour when you reach the top of a rocky hill. The sight that befalls you on the other side is one of hope. But there is also a daunting challenge to be faced.

Turn to **142**.

266

As the beast writhes in its final death agony on the black stone floor, the portal in the east wall clicks open to reveal a corridor beyond. You quickly dash through the secret door just as it crashes shut.

Turn to **209**.

267 – *Illustration XV (overleaf)*

Covering your nose with your cloak, you cautiously approach the dead beast. The sharp smell of its fetid black blood makes your stomach churn, but you are determined to press on. Then you notice a large saddlebag strapped to its chest. Opening the bag, you find a Message written on an animal skin.

Deeper in the bag is a Dagger. You may keep both the message and the Dagger if you wish.

You leave the body and continue eastwards along the path.

Turn to **125**.

268

You black out for only a few minutes before you are revived with a measure of strong spirit. Feeling wary but thankful to be alive, you lean on the shoulders of the King's men and you stagger towards the outer defences.

Turn to **288**.

XV.   Opening the bag, you find a Message

269

The madman lies dead at your feet. Two soldiers soon appear at the doorway and immediately congratulate you. They tell you that he was an escaped lunatic whom they had been tracking for the last two days. One of the soldiers gives you 10 Gold Crowns reward money and offers to escort you to the citadel.

If you accept his offer, turn to **314**.

If you would prefer to trust your own sense of direction, turn to **7**.

270

You hear the angry cries of the enemy drift across the lake. You must leave here before more Kraan appear. You mount your steed and push on further into the forest.

Turn to **21**.

271

You feel very weak. The poison of the snake has entered your bloodstream and you can feel the muscles of your body involuntarily tightening and relaxing. Your legs suddenly collapse beneath you and you feel the slimy water of the marsh close over your head.

Your life ends here.

272

Keeping a watchful eye on the sky above, you move quickly along the track. You recall that this route leads to Fogwood, a small cluster of huts that have been used by a family of charcoal burners for nearly fifty years. After twenty minutes you reach the edge of a clearing where the huts are grouped in a small circle. There is no sign of the usual mist of wood-smoke which gives Fogwood its apt name, and the huts are unusually quiet.

If you have the Kai Discipline of Tracking, you may turn to **134**.

If you do not possess this skill, you prepare your weapon and stealthily approach the huts. Turn to **305**.

273

The outer fieldworks of the city can now be seen. Drawn across the river is a line of barges chained together to form a floating barricade. You can also see soldiers running along the log walls of the field-works, and you can hear the faint noise of battle drifting from the west.

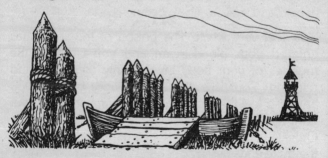

If you wish to approach the barges, turn to **179**.
If you wish to take cover in the trees, turn to **51**.

274

In your haste to avoid the enemy, you catch your foot in a tree root and you are pitched head over heels in a tumble of dust and leaves. You quickly get to your feet and, crashing through the undergrowth at the base of the hill, you run into the forest. You have been running for nearly ten minutes when you discover that you have lost your Weapon(s). Well, at least you still have your life and your Backpack. Wiping the grime from your face, you push on through the trees ahead.

Turn to **331**.

275

You have followed this twisting track for about twenty minutes when you hear the beating of wings high above the trees. Looking up you see a large Kraan approaching from the north, its huge black wings casting a gigantic shadow on the trees below.

On its back are two creatures armed with long spears. They are Mountain Giaks – small ugly creatures full of hatred and malice. Many centuries ago, their ancestors were used by the Darklords to build the infernal city of Helgedad, which lies in the volcanic wastelands beyond the Durncrag mountain range. The construction of the city was long and tortuous, and only the strongest of the creatures survived the heat and poisonous atmosphere of Helgedad.

Quickly you dive for the shelter of a large fern tree as the Kraan passes overhead. With heart pounding, you pray that your quick reactions have saved you from being spotted.

Pick a number from the *Random Number Table*.

If the number you have picked is *0–4*, turn to **345**.
If the number is *5–9*, turn to **74**.

276

Reaching for your Axe you manage to hack your way through the tangle of wood and twisted branches to the clearer forest beyond. Your cloak is torn in several places and your right leg is badly bruised above the knee.

Lose 1 ENDURANCE point and turn to **213**.

277

When you awake, you find yourself lying at the foot of a steep slope in a tangle of tall grasses. Your Backpack and Weapon are missing and your head aches. You cannot tell how long you have been unconscious, but you realize that you must not delay in pressing on with your mission.

Standing up, you see your Backpack is intact but the Weapon is broken in two and is now useless. Remember to cross it off your *Action Chart*. (If you have more than one weapon, only one of them is broken – you may choose which one it is.) You quickly pick up your Backpack and move off into the trees ahead.

Turn **113**.

278

You quickly leave the path and gallop off along the track heading towards the capital. When you reach the point where the Doomwolves stopped, you can see just beyond a meadow the main highway which runs from the northern port of Toran to Holmgard. You should reach the capital by morning.

Turn to **149**.

279

You clamber over the loose rocks and into the mouth of the cave, and then quickly turn to push a large rock over the entrance.

After a few minutes you see the Giaks on the rocky ledge outside, their evil yellow eyes furtively searching every crevice of the hillside. They are so close that you feel sure that they must spot you any second now.

Pick a number from the *Random Number Table*.

If the number you have picked is *0–6*, turn to **112**.
If the number is *7–9*, turn to **96**.

280

As you begin your climb, you hear the beat of wings approaching from the west. Kraan! By the noise they are making you estimate there are at least ten, perhaps more. You curse your bad luck, for the hillside offers no cover from the sky. If you are attacked during this difficult climb, you will find it nearly impossible to fight back and remain upright at the same time.

> If you decide to draw your weapon and remain completely still, in the hope that the Kraan will not spot you, turn to **327**.
>
> If you decide to quickly descend the hillside and take cover in the tunnel, turn to **170**.

281

As you race through the trees you can hear the horrible cackle of the Giaks close behind you. Soon the trees start to thin out and directly ahead you can see a rocky hillside.

> If you break cover and climb up the hill, turn to **311**.
>
> If you change direction and continue your run through the forest, turn to **77**.

282

Looking above the heads of the crowd, you notice that one of the shops opposite the main gate is the timbered surgery of a city physician. Suddenly, a bold plan springs to mind. Bracing yourself against the tide of bodies, you struggle across to the other side of the street. You quickly enter to find that there is no sign of life, apart from a brightly coloured parrot in its cage by the window.

Taking a selection of small bottles you slip on a white surgeon's cloak, and fight your way back to the main gate. 'An emergency!' you bluff, as guards stop and question you. 'It's the royal cook's wife . . . she's having a baby.'

The guards hesitate for a moment, but you assure them that the matter is most urgent and they decide to let you in. One of the great doors swings open about two feet, and you are roughly pushed through the narrow gap into the courtyard beyond.

Turn to **11**.

283

You are only ten feet or so away from the robed stranger when the raven squawks a warning to its master who instantly spins around. You are frozen in your tracks by the hideous apparition of a Vordak, a lieutenant of the Darklords and one of the undead. You must fight him.

Due to the surprise of your attack, you may add 2 points to your COMBAT SKILL for the *first* round of combat *only*.

Unless you have the Kai Discipline of Mindshield, deduct 2 points from your COMBAT SKILL for the second and subsequent rounds of fighting, for the creature is attacking you with the power of its Mind-force as well as with a large black mace!

Vordak: COMBAT SKILL 17   ENDURANCE 25

If you win, turn to **123**.

284 – *Illustration XVI (overleaf)*

Your passage through the Graveyard will not be easy, for the ground is broken and covered with a thorny Graveweed. This wicked briar tears your cloak and cuts your legs. The air hangs heavy and still. Foul gases seep from open crypts and the haunting murmur of distant whispering fills your ears.

Carefully, you approach a gap between two ancient pillars, and part the Graveweed with your cloaked hand. Suddenly, the ground collapses beneath you and you fall in a tumble of earth and stone.

Turn to **71**.

285

With a sickening thud, the chunk of marble cracks open the back of the Giak's head. The creature drops to its knees and slowly falls forward, down to the ruins below. Elated by your skill, you race forward to aid the young wizard.

Turn to **325**.

286

Messengers of death – and ones eager to deliver their news – the Doomwolves surround and then attack you. Valiantly you fight, but it is to no avail for there are too many of them.

As your life's blood seeps away and eternal dark approaches, the last sight you remember is the glint of sunlight on the spires of Holmgard.

You have failed in your mission.

287

The track soon disappears completely into a tangle of thorny brambles and low-branched fir trees.

If you decide to return to the junction and head east, turn to **13**.

If you decide to hack your way slowly through the undergrowth in this present direction, turn to **330**.

XVI.   Your passage through the Graveyard is not easy, the
ground is broken and covered with thorny Graveweed

288

As you reach the walls of the fieldworks, the large oak gates open and you are quickly hurried inside. A sergeant, bloodstained and battle-weary, calls to an officer who turns and recognizes your cloak.

'My Lord,' he says. 'Where are the other Kai Masters? We are in desperate need of their wisdom. The Darklords press us most cruelly and casualties are high.'

You inform the brave officer of the terrible fate of your kinsmen, and the urgency of your mission to seek the King's council. Without saying a word, he motions to a soldier to bring forward two horses. You both mount and gallop off towards the high city wall of Holmgard.

Turn to **129**.

289

The two guards look tired and anxious. They nervously hold their royal halberds in front of themselves, using the weapons to push away anyone who comes too close to the gates. An angry woman attacks one of them, pounding his chest with her clenched fists making him fall against the other guard. All three collapse in a struggling heap of flailing arms and legs. Seeing your chance, you dash forward and pull the large lever which opens the great doors.

You slip inside and the doors close without either of the guards seeing you enter.

Turn to **139**.

290

Inside the long box is a Quarterstaff wrapped in leather. You may take this Weapon if you wish. You close the box and descend the ladder to the clearing below, taking care to use only the sound rungs.

Turn to **140**.

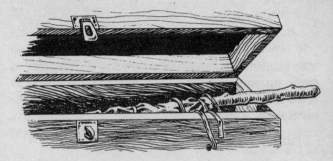

291

The two Giaks lie at your feet, their bodies twisted and lifeless. A quick search reveals 6 Gold Crowns, 2 Spears and a Dagger.

You may keep the Gold and take either the Dagger or a Spear. Remember to mark this on your *Action Chart*.

The Kraan flew off during your battle, and the track is now deserted. You adjust your Backpack and continue your mission.

Turn to **272**.

292

The last thing that you experience of this life is the feeling of being sucked into the void of darkness. No trace of you remains in this world, for you have passed into a realm of timeless existence. You have become a slave of an ancient evil.

Your adventure ends here.

293

With a wave of his hand, Banedon leaves the ruins and you continue your mission, pushing on through the thick woods ahead. You have not gone far when you realize several pairs of yellow eyes are watching you from the undergrowth to your left. Suddenly, a black arrow skims the top of your head. It is a Giak ambush and you must run as fast as you can to escape it.

Turn to **281**.

294

Staying underwater for as long as you can, you finally surface to see the Giaks far behind you. You have lost your Weapon(s) and Backpack but at least you are still alive.

You wade out of the muddy water and continue your journey under cover of the trees that line the right-hand bank.

Pick a number from the *Random Number Table*.

If the number you pick is *0–2*, turn to **230**.
If the number is *3–6*, turn to **190**.
If the number is *7–9*, turn to **321**.

295

You have continued your journey for about fifteen minutes when suddenly a black arrow whistles past your head and embeds itself in a tree. Instinctively you duck and draw your weapon.

> If you wish to remain where you are in order to try and spot the hidden archer, turn to **185**.
> If you wish to run for the cover of denser undergrowth, turn to **92**.

296

You sense something is wrong. With fighting all around and the forces of the Darklords so near, why has this man stayed in the forest? You feel a strange aura of evil about him and decline his offer.

Turn to **90**.

297

Using the skills taught to you by your masters in the art of Hunting, you inch your way through the foliage undetected. In less than a minute you are directly behind, and only a few feet from, the stake to which the ranger is tied. The wood is alight and great clouds of smoke are engulfing the poor victim. You take your axe and run forward, hidden by the smoke. One blow of your axe is all that is needed to sever his bonds, and you pull him free and back into the safety of the forest. As you press on into the forest, you hear the shrieks of the Giaks as they discover that their prisoner has literally disappeared in a cloud of smoke!

Turn to **117**.

298

The head of the bird slowly turns and it curses you. An instant later, it flies off above the trees and has soon disappeared. Shocked by what you have heard you are now sure that the fledgling was a scout of the Darklords and is now probably on its way to inform them of your whereabouts.

If you wish to continue your journey along the track, turn to **121**.

If you wish to leave the track and continue through the forest instead, turn to **38**.

299

You soon realize that you are walking deeper into a wooded marsh. To continue in this direction will be slow and hazardous.

If you wish to continue, turn to **227**.

If you wish to change direction and head towards firmer ground, turn to **95**.

300

You walk for over an hour, during which time you keep a constant vigil for any sign of Kraan in the sky above. You have twice spotted their tell-tale shadows in the sky and on both occasions your quick wits have saved you from capture. You are now very hungry and must eat a Meal.

You may now continue on your journey by turning to **13**.

301

Your Kai Discipline reveals that the west path is a dead end.

You choose the south path and turn to **27**.

302

Pick a number from the *Random Number Table*.

If the number you have picked is *0–2*, turn to **110**.
If the number is *3–9*, turn to **285**.

303

The forest here is sparse and hilly. It does not give much cover from an attack from the air. You move as quickly as you can from tree to tree, to avoid the Kraan but you can hear the sound of Doomwolves close behind.

If you have the Kai Discipline of Camouflage, turn to **237**.
If you do not, turn to **72**.

304

The Gem feels incredibly hot and burns your hand. Lose 2 ENDURANCE points.

You quickly pick it up with the edge of your Kai cloak and slip it into your Backpack. A Gem that size must be worth hundreds of Crowns. But the Giaks are very close and their arrows whistle past your head as you turn and run for the safety of the forest.

Turn to **2**.

305

Through the open doorway of the first hut, you can see the body of a charcoal burner lying face down on the rough stone floor. He has been murdered, stabbed in the back by a spear. All his furniture and belongings have been smashed and broken and not one piece remains intact.

This is the evil handiwork of Giaks without any doubt, for they delight in the destruction of all things. A quick check of the other huts reveals a similar story of murder and wreckage. In the last hut that you search, you discover a Giak Spear – proof of your suspicions. You may keep this Weapon if you wish.

More determined than ever now to succeed in your mission, you continue along the track.

Turn to **105**.

306

The sound of battle gradually fades behind you. Suddenly, you are pulled to the ground. Three Drakkarim have dropped from a tree above. You struggle but it is useless for there are too many of them for you and they are very strong.

The last thing that you hear is the vicious snarls of Drakkarim as they raise their spears.

Your life and your mission end here.

307 – *Illustration XVII*

Your climb is swift and easy. It reminds you of the many trees that you climbed and explored near

XVII.   Pushing open the treehouse door, you see an old hermit
huddled in the corner of the small cabin

308

Toran as a child, when you wanted to pick fruit
or to look out over the beautiful countryside of
Sommerlund.

Pushing open the treehouse door, you see an old
hermit huddled in the corner of the small cabin. A
look of great relief spreads across his face as he
recognizes your green Kai cloak. He tells you that this
area is full of Giaks, and that he has counted over
forty Kraan flying over his home in the last three
hours. They were heading east.

He scurries over to a cupboard and returns with a
plate of fresh fruit. You thank him and place the fruit
in your Backpack. There is enough for one Meal. The
hermit also produces a fine Warhammer and lays it
upon a table by the door. 'Your need is greater than
mine, Kai Lord,' he says. 'Please take this trusty
Warhammer if you so wish.'

You may take this Weapon only if you exchange it for
another Weapon already in your possession, for it is
the only defence that the hermit has against the
enemy.

Thanking the old man, you carefully descend the tree
and continue on your mission.

Turn to **213**.

308

The stable door is open and you can hear the breath-
ing of a horse from inside the darkened interior.
Suddenly, the horse senses your presence and
rushes past, knocking you to the ground. You lose
1 ENDURANCE point.

If you wish to use the Kai Discipline of Animal Kinship, turn to **122**.

If you wish to chase after the runaway horse, turn to **233**.

309

You have taken less than ten paces when the raven squawks a warning to the stranger. Turning to face you, the robed creature utters a piercing screech that freezes your blood and grips your stomach with fear and panic. It is a Vordak, a lieutenant of the Darklords and one of the undead. Within seconds, a host of Giaks appear at its side and attack you. You fight bravely but you are greatly outnumbered.

The last thing you remember is the icy grasp of the Vordak's skeletal fingers as they close around your throat.

Your life and your mission end here.

310

You notice a small faded sign on the wall of a building opposite.

You remember that the royal court sessions are held within the citadel and you are sure that the west road must lead there.

Turn to **37**.

311

The hillside is steep and the earth is loose and slippery. You chance a swift glance over your shoulder and see the two Giaks emerge from the woods. They start to climb after you. About halfway from the peak of the hill, you spot a cave to your right, almost totally hidden by a landslide.

If you wish to hide in the cave, turn to **279**.

If you wish to avoid the cave and continue your climb to the peak, turn to **47**.

If you have the Kai Discipline of Camouflage, turn to **324**.

312

You curse your ill luck. It seems that nature and the Darklords have conspired against you, but it does not shake your determination to reach the King.

Wiping the sticky mud from your clothes, you turn and press on into the forest.

Turn to **299**.

313

Wiping the foul Giak blood from your weapon, you quickly descend the hillside before the Kraan spots its dead riders. Many times you lose your footing on the loose rocks, falling several feet.

Deduct 1 ENDURANCE point for cuts and bruises to your legs.

Turn to **248**.

314

It takes you nearly an hour to reach the citadel. When you arrive you find that the citizens of Holmgard are in panic and confusion. Your escort approaches the armoured guards at the main entrance and tells them of your urgent message for the King.

Pick a number from the *Random Number Table*.

If you have picked a number that is *0–6*, turn to **341**.

If the number is *7–9*, turn to **98**.

315

Wrapped in a bundle of women's clothing is a small velvet purse containing 6 Gold Crowns and a Tablet of Perfumed Soap. You may take these Items and continue your journey.

Turn to **213**.

316

In your haste to avoid the enemy, you catch your foot in a tree root and you are pitched head over heels in a tumble of dust and leaves. Crashing through the undergrowth at the base of the hill, you quickly pick up your weapon and run into the thick forest. The

Kraan is no longer circling above, but you can make out the silhouette of two Giaks on the peak of the hill behind.

Wiping the grime from your eyes, you wince as you discover a large bruise on your forehead. Without delay, you run deeper into the safety of the forest.

Turn to **331**.

317

Instinctively you dive away from the stairs, and land on the stone floor. Your quick reactions have saved your life, for a vast granite block has fallen from the ceiling and crushed the steps, just in front of the lockplate!

Shaken but still in one piece, you get to your feet. A shaft of dull grey light is seeping into the chamber from above, where the stone block was. Through a hole in the ceiling you can see a tangle of graveweed and the cloudy sky above. You clamber out of the tomb and head for the arched south gate of the necropolis as fast as possible. The pointed log walls of the city's outer defence works are now visible.

Turn to **61**.

318

Two soldiers and a sergeant run towards you, their crossbows aimed at your head. As they get nearer, they recognize your Kai cloak and a look of relief spreads across their faces.

'My Lord,' says the sergeant, 'where are the other Kai Masters? We are in desperate need of their wisdom.

The Darklords press us most cruelly and our casualties are high.'

You inform the brave soldier of the fate of your kinsmen, and the urgency of your mission to see the King. He takes you back to the barges where an officer accompanies you on horseback towards the high walls and the main gate of Holmgard.

Turn to **129**.

319

The slimy creature lets out a long, ghastly death cry and collapses. You are near to panic and scramble to your feet, grabbing what you think to be your belt from the jaws of the dead beast. You can see light in the far distance, and you sprint for it as fast as you can. When you finally emerge into the daylight, you fall onto the leafy ground and fight for breath in painful gasps.

Slowly sitting upright, you notice that you are still wearing your belt – you had not lost it after all. What you grabbed from the jaw of the Burrowcrawler was a leather strap with a small pouch and a sheathed Dagger half way along it. You break open the clasp to fnd it contains 20 Gold Crowns. You may take both the Dagger and the Crowns if you are able to.

Feeling a little better now, you gather your Equipment together and push on eastwards into the forest.

Turn to **157**.

320

As you race across the open field towards the wood, a Kraan dives at you and claws your arm. Before you can fight back, it has flown off again, shrieking with cold malice.

You enter the wood, but you have lost 2 ENDURANCE points.

Turn to **264**.

321

You walk for nearly an hour along the twisting river's edge. Beyond the next turn you can hear the faint noise of battle. You carefully climb a steep hillock to get a better view of the area.

Turn to **273**.

322

After what seems an eternity of struggling, you reach the peak of the steep hill. Behind you, above the canopy of trees, you can see the still smouldering remains of the monastery. To the north, a column of jet black smoke rises high into the sky. Small orange tongues of flame flicker at its base. Your heart sinks as you realize that the port of Toran is ablaze.

Suddenly, a piercing cry above warns you that a Kraan is about to attack. It is about thirty yards away and diving for the kill.

If you are going to stand and fight it as it swoops down, turn to **17**.

If you are going to evade its attack and slide down the other side of the hill, away from the Kraan, turn to **89**.

323

From the top of the tower you can see above the trees in all directions. Far to the north, a column of jet black smoke rises high into the sky. Small orange tongues of flame flicker at its base. Your heart sinks as you realize that the port of Toran is ablaze. From the southwest, the wind carries the noise of battle. It is close; no more than five miles at most.

On the floor of the watchtower is a large oblong box.

If you wish to open this box, turn to **290**.

If you would prefer to descend the ladder, and leave the tower, taking care to use only the good rungs, turn to **140**.

324

You pull up your hood and drop down behind the rocks that litter the mouth of the cave. Holding your breath, you curl up into a tight ball, and completely cover yourself with your green cloak. Only a few minutes later the Giaks clamber over the rocky ledge outside, their evil yellow eyes furtively searching every crevice of the hillside.

Then cursing in their strange tongue, they leave the ledge and start to climb towards the peak. You silently thank your old Masters for teaching you the Kai Discipline of Camouflage – it has probably saved your life on this occasion.

If you wish to explore the cave, turn to **33**.

If you wish to leave and descend the hill in case the Giaks return, turn to **248**.

325

Upon seeing you emerge from the woods, the Giak officer shouts 'Ogot! Ogot!' to his cowering troops, who flee the ruins and run to the safety of the forest.

Shaking his mailed fist at you, the black-clad Giak screams, 'RANEG ROGAG OK – ORGADAKA OKAK ROGAG GAJ!' before leaving. Surveying the scene of battle, you count over fifteen Giak dead lying among the broken pillars of Raumas.

The young wizard wipes his brow and walks towards you, his hand extended in friendship.

Turn to **349**.

326

You carefully insert the Key and turn it clockwise. You hear a dull click – the Key works. You lift out the pin, and the large granite door slowly swings towards you on hidden hinges. The grey half-light of the Graveyard floods into the tomb. The exit is overgrown with Graveweed and you suffer many cuts to your face and arms as you fight your way through to the surface.

Looking back, you see the tomb door slowly close and a cruel inhuman laugh seems to rise out of the very ground on which you stand. In blind panic, you race through the eerie necropolis towards the south gate.

Turn to **61**.

327

Within a few minutes, you can see the Kraan hovering over a hilltop behind you. At a quick count you can make out at least sixteen of these horrible creatures, each of which has at least two Giaks riding upon its back. They are armed with long spears and wear tall pointed helmets of dull bronze. You hear the excited grunts of the Giaks. They have spotted you.

You jump for the entrance of the tunnel some twenty-five feet below, but your boot gets caught in a thorny briar and you hang helplessly upside down – weaponless and vulnerable. Fortunately for you the end is swift: As the first Giak lance pierces your heart, death is instantaneous.

Your life and your mission end here.

328

As the creature dies, its body slowly dissolves into a vile green liquid. You notice that the grass and plants beneath the smoking fluid are beginning to shrivel and die. But a large valuable looking Gem lies on the ground near to the decaying body.

If you wish to take the Gem, turn to **76**.

If you would rather leave as quickly as possible, turn to **118**.

329

As you descend the ridge towards the Graveyard of the Ancients, you are aware of a strange mist and cloud that swirls all around this grey and forbidding place, blocking the sun and keeping the Graveyard in perpetual gloom.

A creeping chill seems to penetrate your very bones. Your horse becomes startled and no matter how you urge him on, he refuses to go any nearer to this dreadful place. So you must leave your horse and press on by foot.

Turn to **284**.

330

Fatigued by your exertions, you stop to rest for a few minutes at a fallen tree. You notice a large bundle, beneath the trunk.

If you wish to examine the contents of the bundle, turn to **315**.

If you wish to leave it where it is and continue your mission, turn to **213**.

331

Surrounded by thorny briars and closely packed roots, you see the entrance of a tunnel disappearing into the hillside beyond. It is approximately seven feet in height and just over ten feet wide. As you get

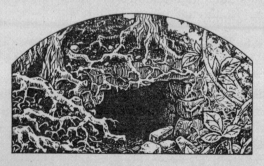

closer, you can feel a slight breeze coming from the inky blackness. If the other end of this tunnel emerges on the far side of the hill, it could save you many hours of difficult climbing. But it could also harbour unknown danger.

If you wish to enter the tunnel, turn to **170**.
If you would prefer to climb the hillside, turn to **280**.

332

You walk for nearly ten minutes along a dark and winding corridor, and then start to climb a steep staircase to a small wooden door. The man presses a secret catch and the door opens. You enter a large, plushly decorated bedroom with a huge marble bath that takes up one corner of the room. The man suggests that you refresh yourself here whilst he seeks an audience with the King.

You quickly bathe and change into some white robes that have been left out on a large marble table. Shortly, the man returns and leads you through a long corridor lined with exquisite tapestries. You finally arrive at a large door guarded by two soldiers wearing silver armour.

You are about to meet the King.

Turn to **350**.

333

You have cut your way through the thick undergrowth for nearly half an hour when you hear the beat of wings high above the trees. Looking up you can just make out the shape of a Kraan approaching from the north. It is one of the monsters that attacked the monastery and on its back are two grey-skinned creatures armed with long spears.

These are Mountain Giaks – evil servants of the Dark-lords, full of hatred and malice. Many centuries ago, their ancestors were used by the Darklords to build the infernal city of Helgedad, which lies in the volcanic wastelands beyond the Durncrag range of mountains. The construction of the city was long and tortuous and only the strongest of the Giaks survived the heat and poisonous atmosphere of Helgedad.

Hidden by the trees, you freeze, keeping absolutely still as the Kraan passes overhead and disappears towards the south. When you are sure that it has gone, you move off once again into the forest.

Turn to **131**.

334 – *Illustration XVIII*

As the stream vanishes up into the rocky hillside, you can see on the track above four soldiers and their officer. They wear the uniform of the King's army.

If you wish to approach them, turn to **162**.
If you wish to use the Kai Discipline of Camouflage and wait for them to pass, turn to **73**.
If you wish to use the Kai Discipline of Sixth Sense, turn to **48**.

335

As you approach, the black bird flies off above the trees and soon disappears from view. You search the tree on which it was perched but find nothing unusual. Rather than waste any more precious time, you continue off along the track.

Turn to **121**.

XVIII.　You can see on the track above four soldiers and their officer wearing the uniform of the King's army

336

You rush into the clearing and take the Giaks completely by surprise. Without a moment's hesitation, you strike out at the one nearest to you. He is dead before his body hits the ground. The other Giaks unsheath their curved swords and attack you. You must fight them one at a time.

Giak 1: COMBAT SKILL 14   ENDURANCE 11
Giak 2: COMBAT SKILL 13   ENDURANCE 11

If you win, you free the ranger and turn to **117**.

337

Just as you remove the ornate pin, a loud crack deafens you.

Pick a number from the *Random Number Table*.

If the number picked is *0–4*, turn to **219**.
If the number is *5–9*, turn to **317**.

338

When you awake, you find yourself lying at the foot of a steep slope in a tangle of long grasses. Your Backpack and Weapon are missing and your head aches violently. You cannot tell how long you have been unconscious, but you realize that time is running out and you must press on. Standing up, you notice your Backpack and Weapon on the slope above. They must have broken free when you fell. You quickly retrieve them and move off into the trees ahead.

Turn to **113**.

339

You quickly sidestep just as a long dagger shatters the glass top of the counter. A swarthy youth is attacking you and you must fight him.

    Robber: COMBAT SKILL 13   ENDURANCE 20

If you kill him within 4 rounds of Combat, turn to **94**.
If you are still fighting after 4 rounds of Combat, turn to **203**.
You may evade combat by escaping through the front door at any stage of the fight, by turning to **7**. ·

340

You gallop forward to meet the oncoming Doomwolf and rider, your Weapon raised to strike. The Giak sees you and unsheathes his scimitar. You must fight both Giak and Doomwolf as one enemy.

Giak + Doomwolf: COMBAT SKILL 14   ENDURANCE 24

If you win the fight, turn to **193**.

341 – *Illustration XIX (overleaf)*

The guards do not believe your story and refuse to let you enter. Your escort disappears into the crowd and you are left alone to find your way in this confused city.

Shocked, and then dejected by such a rebuff, you are carried along by the crowds until you find yourself at the entrance to the Guildhall. It stands at one side of the Guild Bridge which crosses the River Eledil near where it joins the Holmgulf.

XIX.   The guards do not believe your story and refuse to let you enter

If you wish to enter the Guildhall, turn to **210**.

If you wish to search for another route into the citadel, turn to **37**.

If you wish to use the Kai Discipline of Tracking, turn to **310**.

342

As your voice echoes through the trees, the stranger slowly turns to face you. Your heart pounds and your bloods freezes as you realize that the stranger is not human. It is a Vordak, a hideous lieutenant of the Darklords and one of the undead. A piercing scream fills your ears, and the creature raises a huge black mace above its head and charges at you. Frozen with horror, you can also feel the Vordak attacking you with the force of its mind.

Deduct 2 points from your COMBAT SKILL unless you have the Kai Discipline of Mindshield. You must fight this creature. It is immune to Mindblast

Vordak: COMBAT SKILL 18   ENDURANCE 26

If you win, turn to **123**.

343

You are held by the mass of tangled branches and roots. Eventually you free your right hand, grab your Axe and hack your way slowly through the foliage to the clearer forest beyond. Your cloak is torn in several places and your left arm is cut and badly bruised above the elbow.

Lose 2 ENDURANCE points and turn to **213**.

344

You are weak and dizzy. You can no longer feel your legs and they refuse to bear your weight. You try to crawl for the door but the robber jumps on you and pins you to the ground.

Turn to **60**.

345

You pull up the hood of your green Kai cloak and hold your breath as the Kraan circles above. After a few minutes, you hear the frantic curses of the Giaks. The beating of Kraan wings fades, as they disappear towards the west. Your quick reactions have saved you from capture and likely death.

You can now return to the track, by turning to **272**. Or push on under cover of the trees. Turn to **19**.

346

Lodged deep in the rib cage of the skeleton is a Spear. It is in good condition and you may take it if you wish and are able to.

To leave the clearing, turn to **14**.

347

The trees start to thin out, and just ahead you can make out the silhouette of an old log cabin beneath an oak tree. This hut seems to have been abandoned and there is little of apparent value left behind. Opening a small chest near the main door, you discover bunches of twigs that have been tied together with strong twine. One end of the bundle has been coated with pitch. They are Torches. Next to the chest is a Short Sword and a Tinderbox. You may take them and a Torch if you wish but make sure that you mark them on your *Action Chart*.

Closing the door of the cabin, you head off along an overgrown path towards the northeast.

Turn to **103**.

348

Raising your boot to kick away the dead snake, your heart skips a beat as you realize that it was a Red Marshviper. There is no known cure for its venomous bite! You decide that to go any further in this direction would be suicide. Carefully retracing your steps, you eventually reach firm ground and continue on your mission.

Turn to **95**.

349

He is a young blond-haired youth with deep brooding eyes. His face is lined with exhaustion and the grime of battle, and his long sky-blue robes bear evidence of living rough in the wilds. He shakes your hand and bows. 'My eternal thanks, Kai Lord. My powers are nearly drained. Had you not come to my aid, I fear I would have ended my days atop a Giak lance.'

He is weak and unsteady on his feet. You take his arm and sit him down upon a fallen pillar where you listen intently to what he has to say.

'My name is Banedon. I am journeyman to the Brotherhood of the Crystal Star, which is the magician's guild of Toran. My Guildmaster has sent me to your monastery with this urgent message.' He removes a vellum envelope from inside his robes and hands it to you.

'As you see, I have opened the letter and read its contents. When the war started, I was on the highway with two travelling companions. The Kraan attacked us and we lost each other in the forest during our escape.'

The letter is a warning to the Kai Lords that the Darklords have mustered a vast army beyond the Durncrag range. The Guildmaster urges the Kai to cancel the celebrations of Fehmarn and prepare for war.

'I fear we were betrayed,' says Banedon, his head bowed in sorrow.

'One of my order, a brother called Vonatar, had explored the forbidden mysteries of the Black Art. Ten days ago he denounced the Brotherhood and killed one of our Elders. He has since disappeared. It is rumoured that he now aids the Darklords.'

You tell Banedon what has happened at the monastery, and of your mission to warn the King. Silently, he removes a gold chain from around his neck and hands it to you. On the chain is a small Crystal Star Pendant. 'It is the symbol of my Brotherhood, and we are both truly brothers in this hour of darkness. It is a talisman of good fortune – may it protect you on your road ahead.'

You thank him, place the chain around your neck and slip the Crystal Star inside your shirt. (Remember to mark this on your *Action Chart*.)

Banedon bids you farewell. 'We must leave this place lest the Giaks return with more of their loathsome kind to put an end to us. I must return to my Guild. I bid you farewell, my brother. May the luck of the gods go with you.'

Turn to **293**.

350 – *Illustration XX (overleaf)*

You enter the Chamber of State, a magnificent hall decorated lavishly in white and gold. The King and his closest advisers are studying a large map spread upon a marble plinth in the centre of the chamber. Their faces are lined with worry and concentration. A silence fills the hall as you tell of the death of your kinsmen and of your perilous journey to the citadel. As you finish your story, the King approaches and takes your right hand in his.

'Lone Wolf, you have selfless courage: the quality of a true Kai Lord. Your journey here has been one of great peril and although your news comes as a grievous blow, the spirit of your determination is like a beacon of hope to us all in this dark hour. You have brought great honour to the memory of your Masters, and for that we praise you.'

You receive the praise and heartfelt thanks of the entire hall – an honour that brings a certain redness to your young face. The King raises his hand and all the voices cease.

'You have done all that Sommerlund could have asked of a loyal son, but she is greatly in need of you still. The Darklords are powerful once more and their ambition knows no bounds. Our only hope lies within Durenor with the power that once defeated the Darklords an age ago. Lone Wolf, you are the last of the Kai – you have the skills. Will you journey to Durenor

XX.   The faces of the King and his closest advisers are lined
with worry and concentration

and return with the Sommerswerd, the sword of the sun? Only with that gift of the gods may we crush this evil and save our land.'

If you wish to accept the quest of the Sommerswerd, begin your adventure with Book 2 of the Lone Wolf adventures:

Fire on the Water

Pacer
BOOKS FOR YOUNG ADULTS

Pick one up for a good time!

**THE ADVENTURES OF A TWO-MINUTE WEREWOLF
by Gene DeWeese**
(21082-2)
When Walt finds himself turning into a werewolf, one two-minute transformation turns into a lifetime of hair-raising fun!

FIRST THE GOOD NEWS by Judie Angell
(21156-X)
Determined to get a story for the school newspaper contest, ninth-grader Annabelle Goobitz and her friends concoct a scheme to win them an interview with a TV star—with hilarious results!

**MEMO: TO MYSELF WHEN I HAVE A TEENAGE KID
by Carol Snyder**
(21087-3)
Thirteen-year-old Karen is convinced her mother will never understand her—until she reads a diary that changes her mind!

THE TRUTH OF THE MATTER by Barbara Stretton
(21147-0)
When Jenny is unwillingly drawn into Peter's quest to destroy a new teacher's reputation, she finds that the truth is often not what it appears to be.

$2.25 each

Available at your local bookstore or library.

RANDOM NUMBER TABLE

1	5	7	3	6	9	0	1	7	9
3	9	2	8	1	7	4	9	7	8
6	1	0	7	3	0	5	4	6	7
0	2	8	9	2	9	6	0	2	4
5	9	6	4	8	2	8	5	6	3
0	3	1	3	9	7	5	0	1	5
5	8	2	5	1	3	6	4	3	9
7	0	4	8	6	4	5	1	4	2
4	6	8	3	2	0	1	7	2	5
8	3	7	0	9	6	2	4	8	1